TRICK OR TREAT

Ten o'clock came way too quickly for the kids—and not quite quickly enough for me. I bundled them in the minivan, admonishing them not to eat any of their candy until a grownup had gone through it, and headed for the Whitby house. I made the girls stay in the car as I walked Michael, Jr., up to the front door. There was a bale of hay on the front porch with a full-sized ragdoll sitting atop it. Instead of a face, the ragdoll had a jack-o'-lantern for a head.

"Hey, that's cute," I said to Michael.

He laughed. "Mama must have put that up after I left," he said. "Neat, huh?"

And it was. Until I saw the bloody palm of the very humanlike hand of the ragdoll.

"If [E.J. Pugh's] your friend, you couldn't ask for better. If she's on your case, you might just as well give up."
Austin American-Statesman

Other E. J. Pugh Mysteries by
Susan Rogers Cooper
from Avon Twilight

ONE, TWO, WHAT DID DADDY DO?
HICKORY DICKORY STALK
HOME AGAIN, HOME AGAIN
THERE WAS A LITTLE GIRL
A CROOKED LITTLE HOUSE

SUSAN ROGERS COOPER

NOT IN *my* BACKYARD

AN E.J. PUGH MYSTERY

AVON BOOKS, INC.
1350 Avenue of the Americas
New York, New York 10019

Copyright © 1999 by Susan Rogers Cooper
Inside cover author photo by Kate Linger
Published by arrangement with the author
Library of Congress Catalog Card Number: 99-94456
ISBN: 0-380-80532-4
www.avonbooks.com/twilight

First Avon Twilight Printing: November 1999

AVON TWILIGHT TRADEMARK REG. U.S. PAT. OFF. AND IN OTHER COUNTRIES, MARCA REGISTRADA, HECHO EN U.S.A.

Printed in the U.S.A.

WCD 10 9 8 7 6 5 4 3 2 1

To Megan Bladen-Blinkoff,
for always being there

Acknowledgments

I'd like to thank Greg Jackson, M.D., for his assistance with this book. Any misinterpretations of the medical facts are to be blamed on the author.

Also I'd like to thank Vicky Gould, Sharon Strickland, Don and Evin Cooper, my agent Vicky Bijur, and my editor Jennifer Sawyer-Fisher.

One

The definition of hell: A minivan loaded with five children and me. Only three of them were actually mine—two biological and one adopted; the older two, teenaged boys, belonged to my next-door neighbor.

Just because those two weren't actually mine didn't mean I couldn't yell at them as easily as my own three.

"Stop it now!" I screamed.

The minivan was shifting from side to side as we sat at the red light. My two girls, Megan and Bessie, were on either side of the second seat, whacking the sides of the van with their bodies, while my son Graham and my next-door neighbor's two boys, Eduardo and Luis, were in the backseat, rocking back and forth for all they were worth.

There was no response to my demand. Of course. "I mean it!" I yelled. "You're going to tip this thing!"

By the laughter coming from the back, I deduced that was precisely the plan.

"Eduardo, I'm telling your mother," I said, my voice even.

All movement stopped in the van. The light changed and I floored the accelerator, heading into the parking lot of the supermarket.

I've always wondered how Luna, my next-door neighbor, did it. Was it an ethnic thing—that her children would do anything not to bring on their mother's wrath? Or did she harbor her own secret mothering device? I'd never seen or heard her raise her hand or voice; one eyebrow seemed to be all the action necessary. I've always thought she should teach an adult education class: "How to intimidate your children in ten easy lessons."

It was October, coming up on that most hallowed of all holidays—Halloween. In my part of Texas— south central—it was basically still summer. The nights and mornings were crisper than summer, but the afternoon temperatures could still reach ninety without much encouragement. The pools were closed as of the beginning of the school year, but new school clothes weren't out of their wrappers yet because it was still too hot to wear them.

As much of our weather was, we were again in that "in-between" stage. It was three-thirty in the afternoon, school was out for the day, and the sweaters and light jackets necessary for the earlier morning were now either crumpled in backpacks or left in school rooms. As much as I disliked the thought, I had to take all five kids to the grocery store if there was to be any semblance of dinner that evening.

I pulled into a slot only a mile or so from the front door of the Food Giant and herded all five children out of the van. Once inside, the boys headed for the video games while the girls stayed with me.

At nine, Bessie had decided her goal in life was to become a ballerina/nuclear physicist/mommy, and I was selected to teach her the nuances of shopping. Megan, also nine, but whose only goal in life was to get her waist-length hair cut and paint her fingernails green, came along with Bessie and me because Megan loves to talk and the boys will never listen to her. She considers Bessie and me an easy audience.

"So she goes, 'Megan, what are you doing?' and I go, 'Brandy, you have gum in your hair!' and she goes, 'Don't cut it!' She's like screaming, and I go, 'But what do you expect me to do?' and she goes—"

I showed Bessie the relative merits of an eight-ounce can of tomato sauce versus a four-ounce can.

"So I told Mrs. Rudolph, I go, 'Mrs. Rudolph, Garrison shot that rubber band,' and Garrison goes, 'I did not,' and I go, 'Did so,' and he goes, 'Did not'—"

We were in the cereal aisle, discussing Spoon-Sized Shredded Wheat versus Wheat Chex, when I felt a frontal assault on my shopping basket.

I looked up to see Rene Tillery, my son's home-room mother from the previous year, trying to dislodge a wheel of her basket from mine.

"E.J.! Hey! Sorry about that! I swear we need

driving lessons for these damn things. Oops, sorry girls.''

The word perky was invented for Rene Tillery. This day she was wearing tennis whites—a sleeveless one piece with a flouncy little skirt—her dark brown hair pulled into a high, bouncy ponytail. That Rene had been a cheerleader in high school was self-evident. Everything about her screamed ''Rah'' with a capital ''R.'' Rene never turned—she pivoted.

''Hello, Mrs. Tillery,'' Bessie said. She didn't curtsy, but her attitude strongly suggested that if she wanted to, it would be a damn fine curtsy.

''Hi!'' Megan said, turning back to her sister to relay a few thousand more ''he goes,'' ''she goes.''

Rene moved around her basket to grasp my arm.

''Have you heard?'' she whispered, pulling me away from my daughters.

''What?''

''About Michael Whitby?''

I shook my head. The name wasn't the least familiar. ''Who's Michael Whitby?''

''My God, where have you been?''

It was Monday and we'd just gotten back from a weekend in Houston with my parents.

''Houston,'' I said. ''What's going on?''

She pulled me further away from the girls and lowered her voice. ''Michael Whitby! He was a high school girls' basketball coach somewhere in East Texas. He was arrested a couple of years ago on God only knows how many counts of child molestation—with his students!—and went to prison. Well,'' she said, looking around to make sure no one was watching or listening, ''you know the Texas

Parole Board! They let him out after serving only three years of a ten-year sentence! And he's moved to Black Cat Ridge with his family! Into our village!'' she said, her voice indignant.

Black Cat Ridge was divided into economically evaluated villages—we lived in the middle-income village.

''Oh, my God,'' I said, not knowing how I was supposed to respond.

''Madeline Grainey sold him the house, so we're organizing a boycott of Grainey Realty, and Tina Perlmutter think she has a line on where he's working. As soon as we know for sure, we'll see what we can do about putting pressure there. Meanwhile, we're meeting at my house to organize the vigils.''

''Vigils?'' I asked, somewhat overwhelmed.

''We're trying for around-the-clock, but at first maybe just rush hour—as much visibility as possible. And we definitely want to be out there when he's in the house!''

I shook my head. ''Rene, you've lost me.''

She sighed. ''Pickets, E.J. We'll walk a picket line in front of his house until he gets the hell out of Dodge! Luckily there's a sidewalk in front of his house, so that's public access. We intend to walk that sidewalk until hell freezes over or that scum leaves town! Whichever comes first!''

''Who's we?'' I asked.

Rene looked at me funny. ''Concerned parents,'' she said. ''Right now there are four of us in leadership roles, but we are organizing as fast as we can. You're with us, right?''

I sighed. "Rene, I really don't know anything about this—"

She took a step back and looked at me as if I'd just done something unpleasant in my pants. "What's to know, E.J.? A child molester has moved into our midst! Surely you don't condone that kind of behavior?"

"Of course not, Rene. But if he's served his time—"

"Do you have any idea what the recidivism rate is for pedophiles? Over ninety-nine percent! They are not rehabilitatable, E.J.! My God, what sand do you have your head buried in?"

I shook my head. "Rene, it's not that. I'm not naive. This is just the first I've heard about any of this—"

"And you should be as shocked as the rest of us!"

"I am," I said, trying to calm her down. "Of course I'm shocked."

"Where's your son?" she asked out of nowhere.

"At the video games," I answered.

She shook her head. "We're not doing that anymore," she said. "Letting our children run free. We can't afford to now. Keep your children close to you, E.J. Don't let them out of your sight!"

With that she grabbed her basket, pivoted neatly, and was gone.

It's amazing how much wash is generated from two days in another town. I had three loads to do and I wasn't in the mood. Of course, you could put the times I'm actually in the mood to do laundry on the head of a pin and still have room left over for a debutante cotillion. I sorted, fluffed, and folded while Megan stood leaning against the wall regaling me with school gossip.

"James has a crush on Laura, so I go, 'Laura, James has a crush on you,' and she goes, 'No, he likes you.' But, Mom, she always says stuff like that. Why do you think she does that? I mean, you say, 'Laura that's a pretty dress,' and she'll go, 'Oh, yours is much prettier.' That's dumb. Why do you think she does that? And I know James doesn't like me because he never tries to take my lunch money or anything like he always does to Laura, and you know how boys are. They're preverse."

"Perverse."

"Right. So I tell Laura, I go, 'No, he likes you.' And she goes . . ."

I tuned her out. I know I shouldn't. I know I should hang on every precious word in these days when she's still speaking to me. It won't be long before she's buried in her room under a princess phone and blaring music I'll be too old to relate to. But as I sorted laundry I couldn't help wishing that far-off day was already here.

I also couldn't help thinking about my chance meeting with Rene Tillery at the Food Giant. *A pedophile loose on the streets of Black Cat Ridge,* I thought. *But a pedophile who'd done his time,* my other self said. *Three years for ruining how many lives?* my other self said. *He's served his time and he has the right to live in any community he chooses,* my bleeding-heart-liberal self said.

"Mom!" Megan yelled.

I came back to the here and now. "What?" I yelled back.

"I said, how come I can't go to the movies with Laura on Saturday?"

Not having remembered saying she couldn't, or any reason why she shouldn't, I said, "We'll talk to your father."

Megan rolled her eyes and left me to the laundry, which is all I really wanted in the first place.

Michael Whitby
Journal Entry—September 1

I am writing this by order of my court-appointed therapist. He says I need to keep a journal of my thoughts, that these will be private thoughts only I will have access to. But that I must write in the journal at least once a week. I wonder if I've written enough. Ha, ha!

I'm not sure where to begin. Three years of prison has robbed me of my thoughts. Except for my prayers. Prayers, I suppose, are thoughts. More of a conversation, really, with God. In my conversations with God, He has forgiven me. The state has forgiven me—they released me from that God-forsaken hole.

If God and man can forgive me, why can't my wife? She took vows, swore before God and man that she would cherish and obey me, in good times and bad times, forever. I may have my faults, but I haven't forgotten my vows!

What happened, those girls, I take full responsibility for that. I must. I told the parole board that I took full responsibility for my actions. And that was the truth. But I can't see that I'm totally responsible. It takes two, right? I'm not the one who was running around in skimpy shorts, breasts hanging out for all the world to see. Tramps, all of them, tempting me, teasing me!

And speaking of blame—where does my wife stand in all this? If Arlene had ever been there for me, really been there, maybe none of this would have happened!

But I take responsibility for my actions. I'm not a bad man, God knows. I'm a good Christian and I take my faith seriously. A good Christian, a family man, college educated! And I end up in prison! It doesn't make sense, but little in this humanistic world makes sense.

I'm a good father to Mikey, no matter how Arlene tries to turn him against me! I'll not have that! I am the man in this family and Arlene better remember that!

She's more concerned with what her family will think, what the neighbors think, than worrying about her husband—like a good Christian wife should! Everything she does for me, from cooking to cleaning to whatever, I can see it in her face, see the hatred. It's against God's law for a wife to behave like that to her husband! Arlene needs some straightening out, and I'm just the man to do it! A wife is to be subservient unto her husband, not look at him like he's some kind of rabid animal!

She needs to see the situation as it truly is—if she had been there for me, if she had fulfilled my needs as she was supposed to, none of this would have happened. And if you ask me, they put the wrong person in prison!

That's not to say I don't take responsibility for my actions. God knows I do, and by His will I will seek His forgiveness. I don't need anyone else's.

"Who's Michael Whitby?"

"My sentiments exactly," I said to my husband. "Rene waylaid me in the Food Giant, screaming about this pedophile who's moved into the neighborhood."

Willis put his book down and looked at me. "A pedophile here? On what street?"

I shrugged. This information I didn't have.

"In our village, you say?"

"That's what she said."

"And this doesn't bother you?" Willis asked, hitching himself up to lean his back against the bed's headboard.

"Well, yes, of course it bothers me. But—"

"But what? What are we going to do about it?" Willis demanded.

"Do about it?"

"Is *anything* being done about it?" he bellowed.

"Hum. Well. Yes. Rene's leading a vigil-slash-protest, then, of course, there are the boycotts."

"Who is she boycotting?"

"Grainey Real Estate. They sold Whitby the house."

Willis sighed. "Shouldn't waste their energy there. By law she had to sell him the house."

"Explain that to Rene Tillery, will you?" I said,

snuggling up to my husband, ready for the lights to be off and the discussion to be over.

"When I see her I will," Willis said, snapping off the light.

There was something in his tone that alerted me. "When you see her?" I asked. "When will that be?"

I could feel him shrug. "Tomorrow I hope. When we go sign up for the vigils."

I wondered idly if that "we" meant, as they say in Texas, my husband had a turd in his pocket.

Michael Whitby
Journal Entry—September 12

We have to relocate. Fine. They don't want me here—I don't want to be here. Even some of the congregation at our church are looking at me funny! The true Christians, the ones who truly know God, they understand and back me, knowing that a true Christian forgives a sinner his sin. And, yes, I sinned. I allowed myself to be tempted by the harlots in my classes. But God has forgiven me—why can't everybody else?

Arlene says she keeps getting threatening phone calls and blames it all on me. I'm not making the phone calls!

Now we have to move, which could be a major hassle. I've got to go through the parole board, get permission, they'll find us someplace, and help me line up a job. So that should be okay.

I won't be able to be a coach any longer. So fine. Like that was my life's work or something. Standing around watching a bunch of tramps teasing me. Always teasing me with their shorts and their butt wiggles. I sure don't need that.

And I sure don't need Arlene's long, pathetic face watching my every move. The woman doesn't trust me. I've tried to explain to her how it wasn't my fault. She still doesn't trust me. She's obviously forgetting her vows again. I think we need a prayer session tonight. I think Arlene needs to get on her knees before God and ask His forgiveness for the way she's been treating me!

I'm having fantasies about a small, beautifully decorated one-bedroom apartment. It's clean. Always clean because I'm a well-heeled career woman and can afford a cleaning lady. I'm not actually in my apartment as much as I want to be because of my career demands during the day, and the gallery openings and concerts, and dinner and drinks in the evening. Sometimes with career women friends, but sometimes with gray-haired, distinguished older gentlemen, and occasionally an artistic younger man. The men all want me, the old and the young, of course. Physically and emotionally. I may give in occasionally physically—but never emotionally. I don't have time for such encumbrances. I'm a career woman. I have to travel to New York next week for the betterment of my career. Maybe there I'll meet a French expatriate artist living in a million-dollar loft in the Village, who will, of course, want to ravage my body—and my soul—in that order. He of course can have my body—

Then I remember I'm supposed to be writing this

stuff, not daydreaming about it. I write romance novels, the category variety, and sometimes, as silly as they can get, the lives my heroines lead look pretty damned good in comparison to my own.

I love my kids, my husband, my house, my dog, and my cats. Really.

But for the first time in my life I can see the appeal of long visits to a sensory deprivation tank.

Lately I've been feeling jumpy, fidgety. You know, that pre-PMS, I'm-going-to-start-any-day kind of fidgety. But I've been feeling like this for weeks. Three weeks to be precise. Ever since I was supposed to start my period.

I'm three weeks late.

This doesn't mean anything. Really. I've been late before. Twice. Of course, both times I was pregnant, but that doesn't mean anything.

A sensory deprivation tank is looking better and better. I just wish I'd thought about it a few weeks back, say ten minutes before Willis asked, "It's okay if you forgot just one little pill, right?"

Two

"**I think I'm** pregnant," I said.

Elena Luna, my next-door neighbor, and I were having lunch at the Hamburger Hut two blocks from the police department where she worked as a detective.

"You're insane," she said.

"It wasn't planned!"

"Then you're stupid," she said, picking up her hamburger and stuffing it in her face.

"Excuse me, Miss Two Kids in Two Years—"

"I admit I was stupid," she said, then grinned. "But that was years ago and no more kids, right?"

I rolled my eyes. "Kinda hard with your husband in prison, Luna."

Elena Luna had met Eddie Luna when she had joined the Marines at eighteen. They married and when she was pregnant with Luis, their second son, Eddie, a troublemaker of long standing, had gotten into a fight at an off-base bar. The other guy hit him first, but in hitting him back, the guy had fallen and cracked his skull. Unfortunately the other guy was an out-of-uniform marine officer. Eddie ended up serving a full twenty years in Leavenworth, where Elena and the boys took their yearly vacation. Besides Willis and me, only the police chief, Elena's boss, knew about this.

She grabbed one of my french fries, having depleted her own store of them. "Maybe you should consider having Willis put away for a while."

"This isn't funny," I said.

"What does Willis have to say?" Luna asked.

I started stuffing my face with french fries. After all, I was probably eating for two.

"Pugh? What does your husband say about this?"

I was busy washing all those french fries down with a large Diet Coke.

"Oh, my God. You haven't told him," she said.

"I'm not sure yet," I said.

"There's this new invention, Pugh. It's called a home pregnancy test. Try it."

"I hear they're not terribly accurate," I said.

"I hear they're pretty damned accurate," Luna said.

"So what do you know about Michael Whitby?" I asked.

"Changing the subject won't get you out of swollen breasts and hemorrhoids, you know?"

I waved her away. "I don't want to talk about

that now. What do you know about this Whitby character?''

Luna shrugged. "He's moved into our village. It's his right. Not a damn thing we can do about it. He registered with us like he's supposed to. The community has been informed like they're supposed to be." She shrugged again. "Not a damn thing we can do."

"How bad is he?" I asked. "I mean, was this an isolated incident, or—"

"Five girls in a two-year period. That we know of. When there are that many that come forward, there are usually a bunch who don't. It's like an iceberg. What you see on top is quite often the smallest portion."

"Someone said the recidivism rate on pedophiles—"

Luna laughed. "Honey, you got the lingo down, don't you? Recidivism my ass. They do it again, plain and simple. Some people say it's a sickness. They can't stop themselves. Me—I say they're devils. They're evil. Cutting off their whackers doesn't do any good either—they'll find some other way to hurt a kid. They should be killed," she said, "every damn one of 'em."

I pushed the chair back from the table. "Jesus, Luna," I said. "Don't beat around the bush!"

"What? I'm being too blunt? You want me to say that sending these pigs to prison teaches them to stop doing what they like to do? Uh-uh. Doesn't work that way. Eddie said in Leavenworth, they get one of those guys, half the time he comes out of there in a box. Guys in there for murder, rape, whatever, even they think these guys are scum. What are we supposed to do with 'em out here? Say 'hey' in the Food Giant? Sit next to 'em in church? Let 'em coach our Little League?''

"What's the particular story on Whitby?" I asked.

"Likes teenaged girls. Barely teenaged. Thirteen, fourteen-year-olds. No extreme force; talked his way in. Never physically hurt one of the kids—if you don't consider what he did do hurtful. Sorry, but I do."

I shook my head. "No, I agree with you. Rape is rape—whether it's done with a gun or words. It's hard for a thirteen-year-old to say no to a figure of authority."

"Who's got more authority than your coach?" Luna shook her head. "I played basketball all four years in high school. I was real good too. Was all-state my senior year. If my coach had told me to walk naked down Main Street, I'da said what time. I might not've listened to my mama or my daddy half the time, but I always listened to Coach. I guess I was just damn lucky she was a good woman."

I nodded my head. "I had an English teacher like that. He was the reason I wanted to become a writer. The thing is I was madly in love with him my senior year."

"And if he had come on to you?"

"I'd like to think I would have gone screaming to my parents, but I don't think I would have." I leaned back in my chair and hugged my arms around my chest. "I guess I was damned lucky he either didn't like redheads or considered himself an adult and didn't bother with teenaged girls, even when they did have obvious crushes on him.''

"You know they've always been around, these assholes who prey on teenagers, especially girls. And we used to laugh and call them 'dirty old men.' " She shook her head. "How many 'dirty old men' does it take to ruin a girl's life?''

When I got home from lunch with Luna there was a message on the answering machine from Willis. "Hey, it's me. I talked to Rene Tillery a little while ago. There's a meeting at her house tonight at seven. Can you get Mama to come sit the kids so we can both go? Call me back.''

One thing I didn't want to deal with was telling my mother-in-law Vera that a pedophile had moved into our neighborhood. You could never tell which way Vera would lean, but you always knew, whichever way she went, she was going to overreact.

I got her on the phone and asked her if she was busy that evening.

"No, you know I never go out or do anything," she said. "You want me to babysit, I suppose?''

God, the woman can fling guilt like an Olympic discus thrower.

"We have an important meeting tonight," I told her. "A pedophile has moved into the neighborhood." I know I blurted it out this way to mitigate the guilt.

"A ped-a-what?''

"Pedophile, Vera. A child molester.''

"Good God in heaven! Are you sure?''

"He just got out of prison and the neighborhood

is trying to figure out a way to get him out of Black Cat Ridge.''

''Well, take a picture of him and show it to the children. They should know who to stay away from. And put signs in front of his house, so everybody will know what he is! And call all the preachers and make sure they hand out pamphlets with this man's picture! Oh, E.J., y'all gotta do something!''

This is where I was supposed to say, ''But, Vera, he's served his time for his crime. He should be given a chance.'' I didn't say it. I'm not sure if I didn't because I knew it would do no good with Vera, or if I didn't because I didn't believe it.

''I think I'm pregnant,'' I told Vera later that evening.

''It happens,'' she said, not missing a beat as she scrubbed out my kitchen sink with bleach. I used to take this behavior of hers as an insult; now I just accept it and hope she'll start on the bathrooms.

''Willis doesn't know,'' I said.

''No need to get the man involved until you're sure,'' she said. ''Nothing he can do about it now. Men aren't much good with these things.''

''I'm not sure I want to be pregnant,'' I said.

''If you're gonna do something about it, don't tell me. It's against my religion and I don't believe in it.''

I hadn't actually been thinking about that; all I really wanted was someone to say ''poor baby.'' So far I'd picked Luna and my mother-in-law to do the honors. How stupid was I?

''Maybe I'm not,'' I said.

She shrugged.

Willis came in dangling the car keys. "Head 'em up and move 'em out," he said in that cute way he has. (That's sarcasm.)

I grabbed my jacket off a hook by the back door. "Okay, Vera, we'll be back by nine or so. The girls need to be in bed by then, but Graham can stay up until ten. He's finished his homework—he says."

"Go," she said, coming behind us with a hand on each back. "Get out there and do something about that nasty so-and-so. Your babies are safe as houses with me."

Willis and I headed for the minivan to drive to the Tillerys'.

Five years ago, when we first moved to Black Cat Ridge, it was a planned community cut out of the woods on the north side of the Colorado River from the small central Texas town of Codderville on the south. The original developer, a man who obviously had forgotten all he learned at developer school, kept as many trees as humanly possible. Every lot had a stand of live oak, native pecans, or pine. The green-belts were groves of original wood surrounding the homes.

But, of course, that developer lost his shirt, and the project was bought by someone else. Slowly but surely, the woods have eroded with the uprising of a Food Giant here, a Quick Stop there, a U-Store-It where a grove of pines had been, a professional park where the developer worked hard to leave a single tree.

The woods Willis and I had moved to five years before were basically gone now. We live in a subdivision. Just like any you'd see on the outskirts of Houston, or Dallas, or Austin, or San Antonio. We have all of the problems of a big city subdivision—kids in colors, houses too close together, traffic jams mornings and evenings—and none of the amenities. Since we live outside a small town instead of a large city, we have no museums (unless, of course, you want to count the oil rig display in the anteroom of the public library), no theater (except for the Triple Crown, which shows almost exclusively kung fu movies), no ballet (unless you're the parent of a child enrolled in Miss Francis's dance class and get to go to the yearly recital), and no symphony, and no I don't count the high school orchestra whose musical claim to fame is a half-hearted rendition of "The Girl from Ipanema."

Because of a cloudy sky and a weak will, Willis and I got in the minivan and headed the four blocks to Rene Tillery's house, a two-story traditional, not unlike our own, the backyard backing up to what had once been a lush greenbelt of pines and live oak. The woods were sparse now with the addition of a gas station on the street behind the Tillerys'.

Like its mother, Rene's house was perky. There were a lot of fussy wreaths and "project" objets d'art, things that screamed "I came from a kit." Her couches were unmitigatedly floral, and the drapes matched the upholstery. The carpet was springy and the plants silk.

The living room was fairly full when we got there. Of the nine people present, I knew only five—Rene and her husband Keith, a middle-management type who worked at the electric utility in Codderville, and

who had chaperoned a field trip I'd been cajoled
into joining the year before; Max and Carlie Galeana, who we knew slightly from church; and Abby
Dane, whose daughter Rebecca was in Bessie's
class. Abby was a very nervous single mother who
saw bogeymen under the bed at the best of times.
She was sitting on a hassock quietly chewing her
fingernails down to the quick.

We were introduced to the others: Tina Perlmutter, Rene's second in command, and her husband
Davis; and the Bowmans. We weren't given first
names for the Bowmans, which was unfortunate
since it was hard to tell which was which without a
scorecard. They were both about five-five, both
chunky, both wore their equally brown hair in short,
almost identical cuts. Except for the slight protrusion
of breasts, the only thing that separated the Mrs.
from the Mr. were the flowered shoelaces in her
Nikes.

Willis and I sat down, accepting iced tea and
freshly baked cookies, and listened.

Rene stood, balanced on the balls of her feet,
rocking occasionally. In the back of my head, I could
hear the beat, "Rah rah rah." I squelched the urge
to jump up and shout, "Two bits, four bits, six bits,
a dollar."

"Tina has discovered where Whitby works,"
Rene said. "Tina, why don't you give us your
report?"

Tina Perlmutter was a timid-looking woman, with
thin, chin-length, mud-colored hair, about five-foot-
two, in her mid-thirties, and pear-shaped with a rapidly spreading butt. She stood up from where she'd

been sitting next to her husband on the loveseat, dressed in workout duds. But everybody in the suburbs wears workout clothes, whether they know where the gym is located or not.

Her voice was soft and she had to clear it once or twice before she began. "The parole board got him a job with the city parks department," she said, then laughed in a jerky way, "believe it or not. Although they *say* he's only supposed to work in the administrative section and never work in the field."

Rene stood up and rolled her eyes. "That is, until they become short-handed and need him out there. Then he'll be officially allowed to hang around our children!"

There were mumbles and grumbles of the assorted personages, including my husband. I noticed Tina sat down without any fanfare, giving what little spotlight she'd had back to Rene.

Rene bounced on the balls on her feet and clapped her hands together. "People, people! Okay, pressure on the parks department. Davis, any ideas?"

Davis Perlmutter, Tina's husband, a stocky, bored-looking man with helmet hair, clad totally in Nike wear, started at Rene's question. "Ah, pressure? Oh. Well. Phone calls?"

"Good!" Rene shouted, pivoting toward the Bowmans. "Pat? Lee?"

"Letters, faxes, e-mails," the one with the non-floral shoelaces said.

"Pickets outside their building?" suggested floral shoelaces.

"Keith, any ideas?" Rene said, smiling brightly at her husband.

"We could bomb the place," Keith said.

I was the only one who laughed.

Keith and I shared a moment between us while Rene gave us both withering looks. I didn't mind sharing a look with Keith Tillery. He was a big man, the same size as Willis, but with dark good looks. His receding hairline only made him all the sexier.

"Willis, you're here to take this seriously, right?" Rene said, addressing my other half.

"Of course," he said, trying to copy Rene's look as he shot me a glance. "I think all those things are a good idea. But we might also want to hit the parks themselves. So far only the parents in our village are upset about this. All the parents in Black Cat Ridge and Codderville need to know this man has access to our children through the parks system."

"Good point, Willis!" Rene said. I had a feeling there would be a gold star next to my husband's name that evening.

"The more parents up in arms the better," Rene continued. "We need all the bodies we can get for our evening vigils. Willis, you and E.J. are with us on this, right?"

Willis nodded. "Just let us know where and when."

Rene laughed. "Well, where's easy enough! The Whitby house. And how about the two of you tomorrow? We could use you on the five-to-seven shift. Okey-dokey?"

Lee/Pat Bowman (the female) asked, "What's your advice about bringing our children with us?"

"I think it's a great idea!" Rene said. "It teaches the children civic responsibility and it serves as a good visual aid to those driving by. After all, this is *all* about our children, isn't it?''

Rene's husband Keith stood up. "I'm not real keen about my kids holding picket signs outside a pedophile's house. Neither Amber nor Kimberly are old enough to understand what they're picketing."

"I agree with Keith," I said. "My girls certainly won't understand. And if they don't understand what they're doing, they shouldn't be doing it!"

Abby Dane spoke up for the first time. "I don't want Rebecca anywhere near that man!" she said, rather breathlessly. "But we'll need to do something about child care. I'm certainly not leaving her alone while I go picket."

Lee/Pat (the male) agreed. "We're all going to have child care problems. Maybe we can recruit some of the local teenagers into babysitting all the kids at one house. Something like that," he suggested.

"Oh, that's a good idea, honey," his wife said, patting him on the back.

Keith Tillery, who'd obviously been the football player his cheerleading wife had led onto the field back in high school or college, said, "We turned the garage into a playroom last year. It's detached so that would be a good place to use as a child-care center."

Rene beamed at her husband. "Good going, Keith! Great idea! Okay," she clapped her hands again. "We need more bodies! That's everybody's assignment for tomorrow! Recruit, recruit, recruit! Willis, E.J., you'll be on picket line tomorrow night, overlapping Lee and Pat, right?"

The Bowmans nodded their heads.

"Both of you try to bring another couple if you can. Or a single parent if you can't find a couple. Somebody! Recruit, recruit, recruit!"

We all stood, ready to depart. Davis Perlmutter stretched languidly and said, "Hell, it would be a lot easier if someone would just shoot the asshole!"

Abby Dane giggled. "Davis, you volunteering?"

Tina Perlmutter grabbed her husband by the arm, trying to move him toward the door. Davis wasn't having any of it. He turned to Abby with a smirk and said, "Only if you'll hold the bullets."

Tina blushed, Abby giggled, and Keith Tillery, who'd caught my eye again, rolled his eyes and began ushering us all to the door.

We headed for our cars, with me wondering if we'd be given sheets to wear the following evening.

Michael Whitby
Journal Entry—September 22

Black Cat Ridge. In central Texas someplace. My parole officer says they shouldn't have heard anything about my "past" there. I was thinking someplace like Dallas or Houston. Some big city where I could get lost, but no, they're sending me to another small town. It doesn't make sense to me, but not much about any of this has made any sense.

People act like I'm some sort of leper. And the kids are taking it out on Mikey. That's not right! That shouldn't be allowed. Even in Sunday school some of the kids pick on him. So maybe it will be better in Black Cat Ridge. I'll be working with the

*parks department, setting up activities for the kids
at the park. Not that I'll be able to work with the
kids—being contagious and all—but at least I'll be
using my degree.*

*Arlene's upset because she's going to have to
leave her mother. Personally, I think it's the best
thing for both of us. All three of us really. That old
biddy has kept things stirred up ever since I got out.
She's got it in for me. Never did like me. Course I
can't stand her either, so I guess we're even. Sometimes I think she's not a true Christian, even as
much as she professes to be. She certainly doesn't
treat me with any Christian charity!*

*Moving to this new place—this Black Cat Ridge—
is going to be a new start for all of us. The best
thing all around. God has sent us this opportunity
and we are going to make the best of it! Arlene and
I are going next weekend to look for a house. Maybe
we can have some "quality" time together. Maybe
if she's away from her mother for a little while she
can remember what being a wife is supposed to be
about.*

Rene Tillery recruited, recruited, recruited her
next-door neighbors' fourteen-year-old daughter to
babysit in their playroom/garage, supervised by Rene
herself. We took the kids over there at four-thirty,
then headed to Friar Tuck Lane to do our duty.

The Whitby house was a one-story white rock, a
long rectangle of a house with an attached garage,
taking up almost all the width of the lot. It had a
metal roof and a long low porch running almost the
entire width of the house, stopping only at the doors

of the garage. The yard was thick St. Augustine grass, still green and vibrant, well trimmed and edged, and the smell of new-mown grass filled the air.

The Bowmans were already standing on the sidewalk when Willis and I showed up. We were handed signs made by Rene Tillery; nothing as poetic as "one, two, three, four, we don't want your stinking war."

I was well aware that Willis and I were dancing to the NIMBY mambo. People like Michael Whitby had to go someplace, but "not in my backyard." The signs Willis and I were asked to carry said BLACK CAT RIDGE DOESN'T TOLERATE PEDOPHILES! Simple and to the point, I thought. Now the question was: How many of our neighbors knew what a pedophile was?

We did the classic circle walk, waving our signs over our heads whenever a car drove by. Occasionally one would slow down and one of us would walk to the car and answer questions. I left that up to the others; I wasn't sure I knew the answers to what we were doing.

We'd been there less than half an hour when Whitby's car drove into the driveway. I felt like an idiot parading around in front of what I now knew to be an empty house. The driver's door opened and Michael Whitby got out.

He didn't have horns; he didn't even look menacing. He looked like every third guy in Black Cat Ridge. About five-ten, stocky, short blond hair, and a round baby face. He looked like the kind of guy who probably had a nice smile. Except he wasn't smiling now.

The passenger side door opened and his wife got out, looking at us as she did. She was a petite woman with short curly brown hair and a haggard expression. She looked like she had once been pretty, but time and circumstances had done a number on her face. And if looks could kill, someone would be dead—but the look wasn't directed at us, the picketers, but at her husband. If I'd been Michael Whitby at that moment, I'd worry more about what was inside my house than out on the sidewalk.

Then the back door of the car opened and a boy of about nine got out, grabbing his father's hand. "What are they doing, Daddy?" he asked. "Why are they here?"

I looked at that little boy staring at me, the ogre in the driveway. I put down my sign and walked to the van. I drove off, leaving Willis behind.

I was ashamed of myself.

The evening was cool and crisp, the kind of fall night I imagined you might get somewhere in New England. The trees weren't changing color yet, they rarely do. We have a few trees—like pecans—that turn color in the fall, but we're lucky if they get a chance. Usually we get a storm that strips the branches bare before the leaves ever get a chance to change color. The rest of the trees, like live oak and pine, stay green year round, the live oak dropping and growing its leaves continuously.

I hardly noticed the cool, crisp weather. I barely got home in time to run to the downstairs bathroom and throw up. Afterwards, I sat on the cold tile in the half bath and said out loud, "Boy, am I pregnant." Then I burst into tears.

What was I going to do with another kid? What was Willis going to do when he found out? We'd been debating for nine years which of us was going to have the deed done—my tubes tied or Willis's vasectomy. I was adamant that this was his responsibility since having my tubes tied was a major operation, and a vasectomy was just a snip, snip, snip in the doctor's office. Maybe I shouldn't have used the word "snip." The discussion always ended there.

Now it was too late. Not only that, I'd given away all the baby clothes and baby furniture years ago.

I got up and went in the kitchen for a cup of tea. I was a modern, educated, liberal-minded woman. I knew I had a choice.

I was also afraid I knew which choice I'd make, and unfortunately that choice included swollen breasts, hemorrhoids, a new batch of stretch marks, and eighteen years of room and board.

Three

Willis called me on the cell phone an hour later. "Would you like to come get me so we can go pick up our children?" he asked, his voice not terribly pleasant.

"Honey, I hope you can understand why I came home."

"We'll discuss it later," he said and hung up.

This was going to be a pleasant evening.

I went by the Tillerys' and picked up the kids first, hoping to head off a lecture. It worked. Willis got in the van, said hello to the children, and refused to speak to me until after they were fed and in bed.

Around nine, with the girls asleep and Graham in his room reading, I went into the family room where my husband was watching TV. I turned off the set.

"Why did you do that?" he asked, not looking at me.

"Because we need to talk," I said.

"If you care so little about your community—and your kids—that you can't see the merits of—"

"Hold it right there, buster!" I said, standing in front of him, hands on my hips. "Don't you dare tell me how I feel about my kids! You wanna sling some guilt, buddy, you won't like the way I play the game!"

He held up his hands in a gesture of surrender. "Point taken," he said. "I'm sorry. Sorry for what I said about the kids. But I'm mad at you!"

"Let me ask you a question," I said. "Didn't you feel lower than a flea when that little boy got out of the car and asked his father who we were?"

"Whitby brought this on himself," Willis said. "I feel sorry for his wife and kid, sure. But I'd feel sorrier for some other kid if Whitby goes back to his tricks."

"*If* he goes back to his tricks—"

Willis laughed without much humor. "Do you know the recidivism rate—"

I threw my hands up in the air. "If I hear that word one more time, I'm going to scream!"

Willis stood up. "E.J., these people can't be cured. It's been proven."

"So where is he supposed to go, Willis? Where? Do you think any other community will be different from here? What about that little boy? Where is he supposed to go? Do you think he's going to be welcomed at Black Cat Elementary?"

"You know what I wish?" my husband said. "I

wish Michael Whitby would do the decent thing and blow his brains out, that's what I wish. Then his wife and kid would be free of him, and so would the rest of the world!''

"And if that's not an option?" I asked, hands on hips, staring at the man who taught me all about peace, love, and harmony.

Willis sighed. "Just get him out of here. Let him be some other community's headache."

"Not in my backyard, huh?" I said.

"You bet your ass. And if you'd get off your liberal high horse and look at the facts, you'd feel the same damn way."

I shook my head and went to our bedroom, slamming the door behind me, aware that a little more than half of me agreed with everything he said.

Megan was talking at me. It was the next afternoon and Graham was upstairs in his room with Luna's boys and his Nintendo, Bessie was in the backyard having meaningful dialogue with the dog, and Megan was talking at me. I use "at" rather than "to" because "to" connotes a sharing, a dialogue even. This was not the case with my daughter.

I scraped vegetables at the kitchen sink while she tortured me with words. Because nothing more is really needed from me during one of these sessions than an occasional, "Um," or "No kidding?", it took a while before what she was actually saying sunk in.

"So Tiffany goes, 'I'm not sitting next to him,' and Heather goes, 'Gross, me either!' And all the boys are snickering at him and even the teacher acts like he's dirty, and he's not! I think he's kinda cute. And he's nice, too. Well, at least I think he is, but nobody will let him talk or talk to him. I tried, and Laura goes, 'You can't talk to him!' And I go, 'Why not?' and Tiffany goes, 'Because his daddy's a bad man, that's why!' So I go, 'What's that got to do with him?' and Tiffany just rolls her eyes like she's so smart, and Heather covers her mouth like I said a dirty word or something! So I go—''

I turned around. "Megan, what's this boy's name?" I asked.

"Michael," she said.

I could feel color in my face. "Michael what?" I asked.

Megan shrugged. "I dunno. You know him, Mama?"

"I don't know if I do or not," I said, turning back to the vegetables.

"So what did his daddy do?" Megan asked.

I sighed. I wasn't ready for this conversation. I wasn't sure I ever would be. "Help me set the table, okay?" I asked.

Megan rolled her eyes. "Gawd, you always want me to work!"

Michael Whitby
Journal Entry—October 10

It's no different here. It's like they were waiting for us. Knew I was coming before I even got here. People picketing in front of the house. Pressure on me at work now. People looking at me funny. Nobody talking to me! You'd think I was a murderer or something! I didn't do anything! I'm the victim here! But nobody sees that.

I'm supposed to check in with the shrink here in town, Anne Somebody. A woman. I'm worried about relating to a woman. I'm not sure this is the best thing for me, but try to explain that to a parole officer. They're not exactly understanding.

I feel so out of place—everywhere. I made a mistake and I guess I'll be paying for it the rest of my life. One minute I'm a decent guy, a family man, with a good job and the world in front of me. The next I'm a pariah—the scum of the earth. One moment of weakness and my life is over.

I worry about Mikey, how this will influence his life. I never would do anything to hurt my son—he's God's special gift—the light of my life. But sometimes at night I lie awake wondering how this will impact his life—impact—that's one of my therapist's words. But it's a good one. Impact—like a bomb going off. Have I set a bomb off in my boy's life?

It wasn't my fault those girls picked on me. It could have been any other guy in the school! And the girls in this town aren't much better. Some of them have already started in. Like that girl at work and the one behind the counter at McDonald's the other night. Really coming on to me big time. With my wife and kid right there! God, these tramps are everywhere. Asking for it. Begging for it! If they'd sent me to Houston or Dallas or someplace, it would have been better. That little tramp at McDonald's could be just the beginning of a new nightmare.

Michael Whitby, Jr., was in Megan's fourth-grade class. This I found out with a call to one of the homeroom mothers.

"Yes, it's him," Esther Patton said with a sigh. "I don't know what we're going to do."

"It sounds to me like the other children are ostracizing him," I said.

"I know. But what are they supposed to do, E.J.?" she asked. "Half the parents are getting involved with this boycott and picketing thing, and believe me, the kids know what's going on. They may not know why, but the little brats listen to everything."

"Maybe we should have a meeting of the class parents," I suggested.

There was a ladylike snort from the other end of the phone. "If you don't plan on tarring and feathering the boy along with his father," Esther said, "I don't think most of the parents will be interested."

"It's gotten that bad?" I asked.

"Yes, and it's getting worse. One mother called me last week to see about getting her daughter transferred out of the class because she's afraid Michael, Jr., will try to touch 'her special place,' " Esther said.

"Good God, he's nine years old! Has everybody gone nuts?"

"I feel for the kid, E.J., I really do," Esther said. "But I'm thinking the best thing for him is to transfer to a private school. There's a good parochial school in Codderville."

"This isn't fair, Esther," I said. "The sins of the father are being visited upon the son," I said.

"Yes, they are," she agreed. "And there doesn't seem to be a darn thing we can do about it, E.J. I'm just glad to find another person around here who hasn't gone nuts with this thing. But let's face it, child molestation pushes everybody's buttons. Enough that they're ready to abuse another child in an attempt to prevent it."

Esther's son Daniel was the fourth-grader in Megan's class. "How's Daniel dealing with it?" I asked.

"He's getting mixed messages and he's confused, to say the least. He doesn't want to get ostracized by his classmates by befriending Michael. How about Megan?"

I sighed. "Well, Megan loves to get things riled up. She's on Michael's side at the moment. But I'm not sure how much pressure she's going to be able to take," I said.

"Look," Esther said, "ask around discreetly. See if there are any other parents who are willing to be reasonable about this. Maybe we can do something to help the kid."

"Discreetly is the word. I don't feel like having a cross burned in my front yard."

"They're doing what they think is best for their children," she said.

"I know, I know. And I want to do what's best for mine. But I'm beginning to think this is a lose-lose situation."

"Keep me posted if you find anyone," Esther said and rang off.

I sat there staring at the phone. Things were going to get a lot worse before they got better.

*　　*　　*

Willis had recruited the Patels who lived across the street to join him on the picket line. We didn't talk about it much. He'd tried to get Luna, our next-door neighbor, to join in, but she had declined due to her position with the police department. His mother Vera, however, was more than happy to walk the line.

They walked out the door together that evening, Willis not even looking at me, but Vera shooting me a glance. "I'll stay with the children if you want to go," she said to me one last time.

"No, thanks, Vera. You go ahead."

She shook her head and made her usual "tsk, tsk" noise, and was off.

I watched them back out of the driveway in Vera's old Valiant and head down the street, followed closely by Raj and Suzi Patel, who were leaving their two young sons in the charge of Suzi's mother who was visiting from Katmandu.

I felt like the odd man—or woman—out. Which is exactly what I was. I was very rapidly gaining access to everyone's shit list—number three with a bullet, right behind the names of Michael and Arlene Whitby.

There was the obvious reason why I wasn't going on the picket line—my knee-jerk, pinko-liberal political stance—and the not-so-obvious one: the fact that morning sickness was hitting me in the early evenings, just in time to lose my dinner.

And I was spotting. Bright clots of blood that would start one day, making me think that elusive Ms. Curse was finally here, only to leave the next day. I knew I should go to the doctor, or at least to the drugstore for a home pregnancy test, but I was rolling around in a giant case of denial like a dog in dirty laundry.

My new mantra was, "I'm not pregnant, I'm not pregnant, I'm not pregnant." My body was yelling back, "Oh, yes you are!"

I'd just come out of the downstairs bathroom after ridding myself of the last of dinner, when the door-bell rang. All three kids were in front of the TV in the family room at the back of the house, so I headed for the door.

Rene Tillery and Tina Perlmutter, the leaders of the let's-get-rid-of-Michael-Whitby campaign, were standing on my front porch.

"Hi, Rene," I said. "Tina."

"Hi, E.J.!" Rene said, beaming at me, bouncing on the balls of her feet. Her dark hair was in the inevitable ponytail, while the rest of her, like Tina, was donned in suburban jogging wear. "May we come in for just a moment?" she asked, stepping past me without waiting for an answer. "I hope we're not disturbing dinner?"

"No, we've already eaten," I said. Not adding the fact that now I would be able to do it all over again, what with nature's bulimia helping me along.

I stretched my arm out in invitation towards the living room, but they were already headed in that direction. Graham came to the dining room door to see who was there and, upon seeing it was just "women," he went back to the TV.

We all took seats, they on the couch, me on the loveseat, and I asked them, with a smile, "Well, what can I do for you?"

Rene reached across the space between the couch and the loveseat and patted my knee, a pretty frown on her almost-unwrinkled brow.

"We've been concerned about you, E.J.," Rene said. "We saw tonight you weren't with Willis at the picket line, and Pat and Lee happened to mention that you haven't been there the past few times. Are you okay?"

I smiled. "I'm just fine, Rene. Thanks for asking. Can I get you something to drink?"

Rene shook her head. So far Tina had done little more than sit. "Is it the way we're handling this that has you upset, E.J.? We so want the entire community behind us on this, and you are an important part of our community, E.J.! If you have any suggestions on how to make this work better, why we'd love to hear them!" She beamed at me.

I took in a deep breath. "Rene, it's the boy I'm concerned about."

"The boy?" Rene asked, her head tilted ever so slightly, like the RCA dog's.

"Michael, Jr.," I said. "He's being ostracized at school—"

Rene shook her head. "That's the last thing we wanted to happen, E.J.! You know that! That poor boy has suffered enough! If his mother had any sense she'd have divorced that SOB while he was in prison and run off somewhere with her son! But she didn't. She—and her husband—are the ones who have put their child in this situation. Not us. Meanwhile, we have *our* children to think about." She glanced pointedly into the family room where my three sat staring at a sitcom. "We cannot have a man like Michael Whitby running loose in our community! We just can't have it!''

"Where's he supposed to go, Rene?" I asked.

She stood up, no longer rocking on the balls of her feet. Her arms were stiff by her sides, her hands clinched into fists. "I don't really care, E.J. As long as it's not here. I thought a woman with three children, especially a child like Bessie who's been traumatized enough for ten children, would be on our side in this. At least your husband has the sense God gave a bug!''

I stood up too as Tina scurried to join us. "He'll be glad to hear you said that, Rene. Now, if you two will excuse me," I said, heading for the door, "I have things to do. And I know there must be picket signs somewhere with your names on them."

Rene glared at me. "If you're not with us, you're against us. And being up against me in anything, E.J., isn't a pleasant place to be."

I smiled at Tina. "Watch your backside," I said as I gently shut the door in their faces.

Friar Tuck Lane was wall to wall cars. I felt like a traitor—after my self-righteous speech to Rene Tillery—by being there, but had noticed shortly after her departure that Willis had neglected to take his cell phone. Since the two of us had hard and fast rules about the cell phones, I thought it best to take it to him. I asked Luna to keep an eye on my kids, then hopped into the minivan and headed for Friar Tuck Lane.

Four nights before, when I'd briefly walked the line, there had only been the four of us—the Bowmans and Willis and me. Now the sidewalk in front of the Whitby house was overflowing with people carrying picket signs. The sidewalk across the street was lined with gawkers—mostly of the teenaged variety—and the traffic jam in front of the Whitby house resembled Houston rush hour.

I parked a block away, behind a long line of parked cars, and weaved my way through the street towards the Whitby house. Houses up and down the street had FOR SALE, FOR LEASE, FOR RENT signs in the yard—every sign of quick escape except "just take the damned thing."

Car horns honked and kids screamed obscenities at the house. One neighbor was in front of his own house, waving his arms frantically at teenagers who stood blatantly in his flower beds. I could hear him yelling and threatening to call the police.

Basically, it was pandemonium.

I saw Willis in the Whitby driveway, picket sign on the ground, trying to move a scrawny teenaged boy off the driveway. "You're trespassing!" he yelled at the kid. "Stay on the street or the sidewalk or they can call the cops, you idiot!"

"Hey, man, who you calling an idiot, huh?" the boy said, and shoved my six-foot, three-inch, two-hundred-and-fifty-pound husband. I had to agree; the kid was an idiot.

I came up behind them. "Willis, honey, don't hurt him! You know what happened last time you beat up a kid!"

The boy looked at me, looked at Willis, and headed back across the street at a fast clip. Willis grinned at me. "Hey," he said.

"You forgot your cell phone," I said, and handed it to him.

His grin faded. "That's the only reason you're here?" he asked.

"Yep," I said. "We have a strict policy on cell phones, remember? Always keep one with us."

"Yeah, right," he said, clipping the phone to his belt loop. "Thanks."

The front door opened and Arlene Whitby came running out. "Go away!" she screamed. "All of you just go away!"

"No, bitch, you go away!" one of the teenaged boys from across the street shouted. Then he ran across the street and threw something at Arlene Whitby. Two boys followed behind him, pelting the woman with rocks.

Arlene fell. I ran towards her while Willis wrestled with the boys. "I'm calling the cops now!" I heard my husband yell.

Arlene was on the ground; blood was gushing from a cut on her forehead. I kneeled down beside her and tried to shield her from more rocks being thrown. "Are you all right?" I asked, leaning over her.

I felt an arm grab me and pull me upright. "Get away from my wife!" Michael Whitby shouted.

As he picked Arlene up in his arms and carried her into the house, sirens sounded, coming down the street towards us.

Four

Michael Whitby
Journal Entry—October 14

I don't know what I've done to deserve this. God's really testing me. I feel like Job. Any minute I'm going to break out in boils! Arlene had to have twelve stitches in her head from those people last night. And is she ever going to let me forget it? Absolutely not. Like this is all my fault! When is the woman ever going to take some responsibility? I've taken responsibility for my part in this. I was weak. I admit that. I let those tramps seduce me. I admit that. I've asked God for forgiveness and He's given it to me. Why can't my own wife? And why can't she see how she played a part in this? If she'd been a decent wife, if she'd fulfilled my needs, then I wouldn't have been so susceptible to those little tramps! Then they wouldn't have been able to get me in their clutches!

I'm trying to be a good husband, but sometimes Arlene makes it difficult. I did what a husband is supposed to do last night—I came to her rescue, protecting her from those people who were hurling rocks and epithets at her. But did she appreciate it? Did she hold me, cling to me, thank me for saving her? No. She just looked at me as if I'm dirt.

Sometimes I'd wish she'd just leave me. But then she'd take Mikey, and I won't allow that. A boy belongs with his father. Even a father who made a mistake in his life. I guess all fathers have really, except for the true Father. Arlene needs to be reminded that God only made one perfect person—and that was His son who died for our sins. I'm not perfect, but must I die for my sins? Is that what she wants?

Willis and I sat in the Jacuzzi, wiggling our toes against each other's. ''Things got a little out of hand,'' he said.

''A little out of hand?'' I asked, an eyebrow raised. He hates when I do that. That's why I do it. Boys aren't the only ones who are ''preverse.''

''Way out of hand,'' he admitted.

''You realize if Luna wasn't our next-door neighbor you would have been arrested.''

''I don't think it was that bad,'' he said.

Well, he was wrong. Half the Codderville Police force, which oversees Black Cat Ridge, showed up in front of the Whitby house the night before, guns drawn. Teenagers were scattering like leaves in a heavy breeze, and the only people remaining were those who couldn't get their picket signs in their cars quick enough.

An ambulance showed up and took Arlene Whitby and her son to the hospital, while Michael, Sr., stood screaming in his driveway.

"It was him, officer!" he yelled, pointing at Willis. "I saw him instigating the whole thing, getting those teenagers all riled up!"

"Whoa, wait a minute," I said. "He was trying to calm things down, you clown."

Whitby pointed a short, stubby finger at me. "Watch who you're calling names!"

Willis took that moment, of course, to loom forward menacingly, which got him pulled aside by two uniforms, while a third took a stance between Whitby and myself.

"Okay, folks, let's break this up," the uniform said.

"Break it up!" Whitby shouted. "These people are trespassing! They attacked my wife! They're here every night! And you people don't do a thing—"

"Watch it!" the uniform said, raising up to his full height, which was head and shoulders taller than Whitby.

"I'm not afraid of you!" Whitby postured. "Get these people out of here! And do something about this! I want someone arrested for attacking my wife!"

"They were kids and they're long gone, Mr. Whitby," the uniform said, the "Mr." said with a hint of derision. "Seems like maybe they don't want you here," the officer said, and smiled.

I turned away and headed for where the other two uniforms were holding my husband. I noticed the Bowmans were long gone, as was my mother-in-law, whose ancient Valiant was no longer parked at the curb.

"Honey," I said, coming up to Willis, "can we go home now?"

"Ma'am," one of the officers said, "I think your husband needs to come to the station—"

"Hey, Bob," I heard over my shoulder, and turned to see Luna standing there. Behind her was her car, loaded to the gills with her kids and mine. "Heard over the radio you had my neighbor in custody. Willis, what *have* you done now?" she asked, grinning.

The officer let go of his hold on Willis's arm. "You vouch for this guy?" he asked Luna.

"Sure. He's harmless," she said.

The uniform who had been talking to Whitby and me was walking Whitby to his car for an escort to the hospital.

The other two officers waved at Luna and left, leaving the three of us standing on Whitby's sidewalk.

And this was what my husband considered "a little out of hand."

"Well, if you had been arrested," I said, nestling down in the warm water and sliding a foot under my husband's very shapely butt, "maybe you could have gotten the family cell," indicating the cell my mother-in-law and I had shared for a few hours a while back, the same one in which my sister-in-law Juney had resided for two days not too long ago. I figure one more Pugh in that cell and we deserved a plaque.

"Very funny," he said, splashing water at me.

"Have you heard from Rene the Magnificent?" I asked. "Surely she's calling this thing off now."

"Ha!" Willis said. "Rocks and arrest deter Rene Tillery from her appointed rounds? Never. I'm sure as we speak she's somewhere recruiting, recruiting, recruiting."

"Losing a little bit of the love affair with Dear Rene?" I asked, in that snippy tone only a wife can use.

"Rene's an idiot," Willis said. "But I still agree with her, E.J."

I sat up in the tub. "After all that happened last night, you still think you should be doing this?"

Willis shrugged. "Ah, hell, that was nothing. I withstood dogs and gas back in the good old days."

"Yeah, well you were younger then and had quicker reflexes. Not to mention you weren't hampered with the weight of a wife and three children."

Willis bristled. "I'm doing this *for* my children, E.J."

"Maybe you should know that one of your children—Megan to be precise—is in the same class with Michael, Jr. And, as far as I can tell, she's his only friend. And she came home crying today because of things the other kids said to her. So how are you helping her with your zero-tolerance stance?"

Willis sighed and leaned his head against the tub.

"God, I hate this!" he said, then went head first under the water.

Somehow, it seemed an appropriate response to the situation.

"Spotting is not a good thing, whether you're pregnant or not."

"I know."

Luna rolled her eyes. "Go to the doctor, for God's sake."

"Yeah, I suppose I should."

We were at Tiffany's Tea Room, a new place that had opened in Black Cat Ridge and served very good sandwiches. I picked at the sprouts on my avocado melt.

"What's with you?" Luna asked, actually setting down her sandwich to look at me.

"What do you mean?"

"I mean, what's with you? You're a pain in the ass, but you're usually not a stupid one. You are acting stupid about this, E.J. What's going on?"

I shrugged. Had I gotten over the fear that Willis would leave me if I brought one more child into our midst? Mostly. Ninety-nine percent of it. But there was still that one little percentage point that kept bopping around in my head. I had to wonder sometimes what my mother did to me as a young child to make me so insecure. Right, I thought, it's always the mother's fault!

Or was it me? Had I already split myself so many ways I was afraid there wouldn't be enough for another child? Or was it simply the fact that I really, really, really didn't want another child?

I sighed. "Oh, God," I said. "I don't want it."

"That's something you need to talk over with Willis."

"It's my body—"

"And his baby," she said. "Don't you think it should be a joint decision?"

I shook my head. "I can't do that. I just can't. Politically I agree a woman has a choice, Luna, but I just can't do it."

"Then what are you saying?"

"I don't know!" I shouted.

All the patrons, mostly female, in Tiffany's Tea Room, stopped talking and looked at me.

"Let's get out of here," Luna said.

She paid for the check while I headed to the minivan where I fell into hysterics.

Luna climbed into the seat next to me and patted my arm, making soothing noises while I cried it out.

I finally stopped and she handed me the box of tissues on the console. I blew my nose and she said, "Hell, babies can be fun, remember?"

I nodded my head.

"And they smell so good," I said.

Luna smiled. "And remember the first time they laugh?"

I nodded my head.

"And that first step," I said.

"Yeah, but if you can, try not to teach this one to talk. It could be another Megan."

I sighed. "I think, whether it's a boy or a girl, I'll name it Lucky."

*   *   *

Rene was tickled to death about the uprising of the other night. She thought we were really getting somewhere, she told Willis.

"She said she was sorry Mrs. Whitby had to get hurt, but that we were obviously pushing some buttons," Willis told me.

"Yeah, the same buttons you'd push if it was an unwanted African-American family, or Jewish, or Asian, or—"

"Oh, for God's sake!" Willis shouted. "Get off your high horse! It's not the same thing at all! I can't believe that you—a woman—can't see this! The man is a menace! Especially to women! Very young women! Have you totally lost your mind?"

"People were throwing rocks, Willis! They hit and hurt an innocent woman—"

"Innocent, my ass! She's married to him, isn't she?"

I threw my arms up in the air. "That means she's guilty of something? By that reasoning, so is the boy! He's Michael Whitby's actual blood. Maybe we should just have him put down like an unwanted puppy! God knows, he could, just *could,* grow up to be like his father!"

Willis stared at me. "You are not acting reasonably," he said, in what I'm sure he considered a reasonable tone of voice. "That man hurts children. He doesn't deserve to be in polite society. For whatever reason, he has been released into our midst. We do not have to take this. We have the right to live in our community without fear!"

I laughed. "Without fear? Excuse me? Do you live in the same house I do? The one that was broken

into by two murderers? The one next door to where
our best friends were murdered in their sleep? The
house that was practically burned to the ground by
arson? The house where a boy's body was left in
our driveway? Need I go on?''

"One has nothing to do with the other," Willis
said, straightening his spine and glaring at me.

"What does that mean?" I asked.

Willis put his hands on his hips and stared at me.
Finally, he said, "I don't know."

Michael Whitby
Journal Entry—October 20

*I had to go see that shrink today. She asked about
the journal. I said I was keeping one but that it was
private and my last shrink said I didn't have to show
it to him and I had no intention of showing it to
her. She got real huffy about it. I called my parole
officer and said I wanted him to find me a new
shrink—this time a man, but he said I had to take
what I got and shut up.*

*You'd think I had no rights! These people treat
me like I'm some sort of low life. My P.O. acts like
I'm just like the scum he usually deals with! I'm
not! I'm not like those other guys. I'm a decent guy.
A family man. One little mistake and they act as if
I'm the devil incarnate! Well, I'm not! I'm so much
more than that one little mistake, but no one sees
that, not even the one person who should—my wife.
I'm a husband, a father, a son, a college graduate,
the first in my family! I'm a coach—and a good one,
too—all state girls basketball two years in a row!*

Does anyone ever mention that when the name Michael Whitby comes up? No, all they ever mention is the mistake. I'm a Christian, I was a deacon in my church, a member of the Jaycees back home. There's so much more to me than that one little mistake.

When will Arlene see that? She of all people should know. But I will give her this—she stayed. A lot of women would have walked out, gotten a divorce while their husband was in prison. But Arlene didn't do that. She fulfilled her Christian duty—she stood by me. I'll always be grateful for that. Does she love me? I don't know. Do I love her? She's a good woman, a good mother, a good wife, in a lot of ways. Although she has failed me many times. I think she's just confused. I know I am sometimes. We need to have an evening family prayer session. All of us, bowing before God and asking for His forgiveness and His guidance. Maybe we can be a family again. I pray so.

I left Graham playing Nintendo with Luna's boys and took the girls to the grocery store. Graham's twelve now and he insists he's old enough to stay by himself, although we both agree he's not old enough to babysit his sisters. According to Graham, he'll never be old enough to do that.

Which is just as well. Graham's idea of paying attention to the girls is to shut and lock the door to his room—with him on one side and the girls on the other.

We made it the five blocks to the Food Giant with only two major fights, and went into the grocery store. We were on the spice aisle, looking for a bottle of coriander to replace the one I had that was at least five years old, when I heard Megan say, "Hey, Michael!"

She was waving wildly at a cart at the other end of the aisle. I looked up and saw Arlene Whitby and her son.

Megan grabbed my hand and started dragging me in their direction. "Come on, Mom! I want you to meet Michael!"

Arlene Whitby stiffened as we approached. Michael grinned at my daughter. "Hey, Megan," he said.

I stuck out my hand to Michael's mother. "Mrs. Whitby," I said. "I'm E.J. Pugh."

She looked at my hand, then at my face. "You're the woman from the other night. When I was hit."

I retracted my hand and nodded my head. "I wasn't with the pickets, Mrs. Whitby—"

"Then why were you there?" she asked, her posture ramrod stiff.

Well, I could have said, "To bring my husband his cell phone since he was one of the pickets," but that didn't seem to be a good idea. I opted for a lie.

"I was driving by and saw what happened," I said. "I'm sorry you were hurt."

"Are you?" she said, staring at me. "Then you're the only one around here who is."

"Mama!" Michael said, grabbing her arm. "This is my friend Megan."

Arlene Whitby smiled down at my daughter. "Hello, Megan. I've heard a lot about you. It's nice to meet you."

Megan said, "Yeah, me too." She grabbed Bessie, who was standing behind me. "This is my sister, Bessie. Bessie, this is Michael, the boy I was telling you about."

Bessie smiled. "Hi, Michael," she said.

Megan said, "Mama, can we take Michael and show him the video arcade? Huh? Can we?"

"Please, Mama?" Bessie said.

I looked at Arlene. "If it's okay with Mrs. Whitby," I said.

Arlene nodded and the three ran off, heading in the direction of the video arcade.

"You aren't afraid my son will ravage your daughters?" Arlene said, still standing stiffly in front of me.

"He wouldn't stand a chance with those two," I said. "I'm sorry for your trouble, Mrs. Whitby," I said.

"Really? Why?"

"Because of the way it's affecting your son. He seems like a very nice boy."

Arlene Whitby visibly relaxed. She smiled tentatively. "He is," she said. "He's a very nice boy." She stiffened again. "But a boy needs a mother *and* a father, no matter what that father may have done. That's my belief and that's what my church teaches."

She was giving me her excuse for not having divorced Michael Whitby. I wonder if she found it as hard to swallow as I did.

"You have the right to do whatever you wish, Mrs. Whitby," I said. "Just like the people in this community have the right not to like it."

"And the right to throw rocks at me and hound my son?"

I shook my head. "No. They don't have the right to do that."

"But they do it anyway," she said.

I nodded my head. "Yes," I said, "I guess they do."

Arlene Whitby started to push her cart away from me. "Mrs. Whitby," I said.

She stopped and turned to look at me, her body tense. "Yes?"

"Why don't you bring Michael over to play sometime?" I suggested. "We live in the second house on the left on Sagebrush Trail."

"Why are you being nice to me?" she blurted out.

"Because you didn't do anything wrong," I said.

She looked at me for a long moment, then nodded her head. "I'll see about bringing Michael by sometime soon," she said, then moved on with her cart.

I watched her walk away, a small, fragile woman with the weight of the world on her shoulders. I didn't envy Arlene Whitby her life.

Five

Michael Whitby
Journal Entry—October 23

*That McDonald's is right down the street from my
office. It's practically the only place to eat around
here, which is the only reason I've been going by
there. That girl—the one who was coming on to me
in front of Arlene and Mikey—she's there almost
every day. She looks too young for that, and I said
so, then she told me she was on a work program at
school—half days at school, half days working. I
don't think they should do that. Kids should be kids,
ya know. They shouldn't have to work. But she seems
very mature for her age. I try to be friendly to her,
but I'm afraid she's getting the wrong message. She
keeps touching my hand and smiling at me. I don't*

*know why these girls keep doing this to me, but I'm
stronger now than I was. I won't let her get me in
trouble, I guarantee you that!*

*It would help my resolve if Arlene would just get
off my back! She's so much like her mother. I
thought we could get away from the old biddy when
we moved here, that at least that would be better,
but no, Arlene talks to her every day! Like I don't
have enough bills with still paying off the lawyer
and all the bills Arlene racked up while I was in
prison! Not only am I in prison, but my wife's on
the outside acting like she had a right to my credit
cards! Running up bills like there's no tomorrow! I
tell you, she needs to be taught a lesson, and I'm
just the guy who can do it. I'll teach her a lesson
she won't soon forget!*

The phone rang about three o'clock. The kids
were out in the backyard terrorizing the dog, and I
was sitting at the breakfast-room table, reading *Parent* magazine and wishing I still smoked.

I picked it up on the second ring. "Hello?" I said.

"E.J.! Hi, it's Carlie Galeana," she said. Carlie
and her husband Max had been one of the couples
at the meeting Willis and I had gone to at Rene
Tillery's house. We knew them slightly from church.

Carlie was a pretty woman who was always battling her weight. I don't think I've ever had a conversation with her that didn't at some time meander
to a discussion of the diet she was currently on.
Until now, of course.

"Hi, Carlie," I said. "How are you?"

"Fine, E.J. How are the kids?"

"Fine," I said, wondering why she had called. Except for a time three years ago when the two of us had been on a church committee together, I couldn't remember her ever having called me. "How are your kids?" I asked, in an attempt to keep the conversation going.

"Great, just great," she said. There was a small silence, then she said, "I was at the grocery store today."

"Oh?" I asked, at first genuinely puzzled. Then I remembered my own trip to the grocery store. "So was I," I said.

"I know. I saw you. I was going to come over and say hi, but I noticed you were talking to Arlene Whitby."

Another long silence.

Finally, I said, "Yes, I was."

"What did she want?" Carlie asked.

"What do you mean?"

"Well, did she approach you, or what?"

"Her son and my daughter are in the same class," I said, and left it at that.

Another silence.

Carlie cleared her throat. "Yes, I noticed your daughters in the video room with that boy."

I could feel the hair on my arms standing at attention. "What can I do for you, Carlie?" I asked.

She sighed. "Jesus, I don't know, E.J. God, I hate this! I didn't see you. I wasn't even *at* the store today! Some neighbor of Rene's saw you and called her and she called me because she said she couldn't talk to you because you were being a pain in the ass, and thought maybe I could since we went to church together and, shit, I don't know!''

''And she wants to know if I'm consorting with the enemy?''

Carlie sighed again. ''Something like that. Look, E.J., you don't have to tell me anything. I don't care. I hate the fact that this man has moved into our neighborhood, but I'm not all that crazy about some of Rene's ideas, either. My God, she was actually thrilled that somebody hit Arlene Whitby with a rock!''

''Carlie, I'm as confused as you are. I don't want that man here either, but I don't know what to do about it. All I know is ostracizing the boy and beating up on the wife is not the way to do it!''

''I know, I know. God, this is awful. The whole community's going nuts. And you know, E.J., it's not Rene's fault. It's Whitby's fault! It's all Whitby's fault and I wish the asshole would just die!''

''Carlie—''

''Look, I've got to go. I'll just tell Rene she was talking to you about homeroom class, okay? That should pacify her. Bye, E.J. And I'm sorry.''

She hung up before I had a chance to say goodbye.

''You're not going back over there?'' I asked Willis that evening after dinner.

He was grabbing his coat and heading for the back door.

He turned and looked at me. ''Yes,'' he said very deliberately, ''I am going back to picket. Wanna come?''

"Only if I can bring my own sign," I said.

"And what would your sign say?" he asked.

Well, he had me there. I had no idea what my sign would say. What could it possibly say that would stem the tide of violence I could see coming?

"Just go," I said. I kissed him on the mouth. "Stay out of trouble."

Michael Whitby
Journal Entry—October 25

Her name's Mandy and she's fifteen, which is way too young to be working, as far as I'm concerned. I took a late lunch today, so the store was almost empty and we had a chance to talk. On my way home tonight I drove by there and saw her walking home. She was in front of me in her uniform, her butt swaying back and forth and her trying to act like she didn't know I was back there watching her. When I pulled up beside her and offered her a ride, she said no, but she was smiling at me. I wasn't comfortable with the way she was smiling at me, but I'm the adult here and the one who has to nip this in the bud. There's no reason why we can't be friends, but she can't expect more than that from me.

I was in bed reading when Willis came home that night. He leaned over and kissed me then headed for the bathroom.

"How'd it go?" I asked.

I could hear him brushing his teeth. "Okay," he said, spitting. "Not near as much excitement as the other night."

"That's good," I said.

He crawled in naked beside me. "Ooo, it must be cold out there," I said, feeling his freezing thigh rubbing up against mine.

"Um-hum, make me warm," he said, pulling me toward him.

"I'm trying to read," I said.

"Um, I'll read to you, baby," he said.

I looked at him. "How can you make reading sound dirty?"

"It's a gift," he said, nuzzling my neck.

"So answer me this. Does Rene do any of her own dirty work?"

He rolled over onto his own pillow and sighed. "All I want is to get laid," my husband said. "Do we have to talk politics?"

"Very romantic," I said. "I mean it. Does she ever hold any picket signs?"

"She came by tonight to see how we were holding up, but just as our general, not one of the actual troops."

"Who all was there?"

"The Bowmans—"

"Have you figured out which is which yet?" I asked.

"I think *he's* Pat. But don't quote me on it. Anyway, they were there, and poor Keith—"

"Poor Keith?"

"Yeah, I get the impression he wants to be there about as much as you do. You're just damn lucky you're not married to Rene—"

"My mother would frown on that—"

"You know what I mean," he said, kneeing my

leg. "The guy strikes me as the noninvolvement kind."

I sat up and looked at my husband. "Is that what you think I am?" I accused.

Willis laughed. "I would never accuse you of noninvolvement, Eeg. You get involved in more things than you should. No, believe it or not, I do understand your reasoning on this, honey. I just don't agree with it—"

"How can you believe in the rights of the individual and still do—"

"What about free speech?" Willis countered. "Besides, I'm not trying to argue with you. I'm talking about Keith Tillery, not you."

I sighed. "What about him?"

"I get the impression this whole thing bores and embarrasses him. That's all," Willis said.

"Well, I can see where being married to Rene would be an embarrassment."

"You've got a point," Willis agreed. We finally stopped talking politics. For a little while.

I woke up around 3 A.M. My pulse was racing and my head spinning. I sat up and had to grab the headboard to steady myself. Then the nausea hit me. I stumbled up and managed to make it to the foot of the bed before I threw up on the carpet.

Willis is a very sound sleeper. He actually slept through two not so minor earthquakes while we were living in Mexico. What he could not sleep through, however, was my grabbing his foot and twisting it until the ligaments screamed.

"What?" he yelled, sitting bolt upright in bed.

"Help," I said, leaning against the bed's foot-board and trying to suppress the dry heaves.

He turned on the light and jumped out of bed, almost stepping in the mess I'd made on the floor.

"Jesus Christ, honey, are you all right?"

"No," I said. "I'm pregnant." Which must have been about the time I passed out.

When I came to, I was on the bed and Willis was bathing my face with a cold, wet washcloth. I batted his hand away.

"Should I call an ambulance?" he asked.

I shook my head. "Not much they can do about my condition," I said.

"You never passed out before," Willis said, again mopping at my brow.

"I was never this old before," I said.

"What did the doctor say?" he asked.

"What doctor?" I asked.

"The doctor who told you you were pregnant," my husband said, obviously trying to hold on to his temper.

"I haven't been to the doctor," I said.

"So you did a home pregnancy test?"

I cleared my throat. "Well, no, not exactly."

Willis stopped mopping my brow and sat down on the bed. "Not exactly," he said. "What does that mean?"

I didn't want to look at him. So far he had not been unreasonable about my declaring my delicate condition, but I had the unfortunate feeling that wasn't going to last long.

"I just have all the symptoms," I said.

"Um-hum," he said. He got up and went to the bathroom, coming back with a towel from the dirty clothes hamper to clean up the mess at the foot of the bed.

"How long has this been going on?" he asked.

"Not long," I said.

His head loomed at me from the foot of the bed. "Exactly how long is not long?" he asked.

"A couple of weeks," I said.

"A couple of weeks?" he repeated. "Like two?"

I shrugged. "Maybe three," I said.

"Three?" he repeated.

"Are you going to repeat everything I say?" I asked.

"You've been having signs and symptoms of pregnancy for three weeks and this is the first I hear of it?"

My pulse was racing again and my head spinning. I laid my head down against the pillow. "I don't feel good," I said.

"No shit, Sherlock," my husband said, then disappeared into the closet. When he came out, he was dressed in jeans, sneakers, and a T-shirt.

"Where are you going?" I asked.

"To the all-night drugstore," he said. "It's time somebody in this room took a home pregnancy test."

I've never been a "pee on command" type of person. I read the instructions several times and sat down with the test stick between my legs, waiting for the inevitable. Finally, I turned on the water in the sink, closed my eyes and thought of waves splashing on a beach, a waterfall, great big glasses of iced tea, anything.

Nothing.

I got up and Willis brought me a glass of water. I sat on the side of the bed, my head spinning and my pulse racing, and drank the water.

"Why is your face so red?" Willis asked.

"I don't know, is it?" I started to stand up and check myself out in the bathroom mirror, but I was too dizzy to get up.

Willis grabbed the water glass out of my hand. "Lie down," he said. He grabbed my hand to help me down, his finger touching my wrist. He stopped and held my wrist, two fingers pressed against my pulse.

"Your pulse is racing," he said. "It's about twice what it should be."

"Thank you, Dr. Spock," I said.

"That's Mr. Spock to you. I'm serious, honey. You need to see the doctor."

"I'm okay," I said. "I just—"

I sat up quickly. "I'm going to heave," I said, trying to make it to the bathroom. Willis grabbed my arm and helped me to the commode.

All the water came out—but not from where I'd hoped.

We crawled back into bed and Willis held me until I fell asleep.

I woke up late. I knew this because the sun was streaming in the bedroom windows and I hadn't seen the sun in my bedroom since—okay, since the last time I'd been sick.

I felt a lot better. My head wasn't spinning, my pulse wasn't racing, and my stomach was empty. But I had to pee like a racehorse.

I made it into the bathroom, grabbed the handy test stick, and did as instructed. Then I covered it, set it on a flat surface, and went into the bedroom to pretend that I wasn't counting the three minutes.

After the allotted time, I went back. There were two red lines in the little windows of the test stick.

I was pregnant.

Six

Michael Whitby
Journal Entry—October 27

*I gave Mandy a ride home last night. She lives in a
trailer park about a mile from the McDonald's. I
couldn't believe her folks let her walk a mile home
in the dark, but then I found out her dad's long
gone and her mother usually goes out with her
boyfriend after work. Mandy doesn't see her sometimes for days. Poor kid. She needs a stable adult
influence in her life. I believe I can be that stable,
adult influence. I'm not the man I was five years
ago. I have the will power now to resist what she
obviously wants from me. I'm going to be her role
model—her teacher—her mentor. God knows
what's in my heart, and that my heart is pure.*

*I've made my mistake in this lifetime, and it won't
happen again.*

I wandered downstairs, wondering where the kids
were. Willis was in the kitchen, cleaning up breakfast dishes.

"Where are the kids?" I asked.

"I took them to school two hours ago," he said.
"How are you feeling?"

I sighed. "I took the test," I said.

He looked at me. Finally, he said, "And?"

I nodded my head.

Willis sat down in the nearest chair. "Well," he
said.

I nodded my head.

"Well," he said again.

I looked at the spilled cereal on the table and ran
into the half bath under the stairs to vomit.

When I came out, Willis said, "I don't remember
you reacting like this with Graham or Megan."

"Like I said, I'm older now."

He got up and went to the phone and dialed.

I went into the living room and laid down on the
couch. I didn't know who he was calling and I didn't
really care. If someone showed up with a strait-
jacket, it could only make my day a little brighter.

A few minutes later Willis came into the living
room. "You need to get dressed, honey. Dr. Colman's going to fit you in as soon as we get there."

"Okay," I said, not moving. I closed my eyes to
keep the room from spinning.

Willis shook me gently. "Here, put this on," he
said.

I opened my eyes. He had a T-shirt, blue jeans, bra, panties, socks, and running shoes. He's a good man, my husband.

He helped me get dressed and we made it to the minivan and finally to the doctor's office.

Marta Colman was a tall, thin, mid-thirties blonde with more spunk than she needed. I liked her in spite of myself. She'd been my OB/GYN for the entire time we'd been in Black Cat Ridge.

Her nurse Rosemary took Willis and me back immediately. She had me pee in a cup, then disrobe and put on the nasty little gown that never comes close to covering my big butt, took my vitals, and left Willis and me alone.

I laid back on the examining table, my feet studiously avoiding the stirrups, and closed my eyes. Willis pulled up a chair and sat next to me, taking my hand in his.

Five minutes later, Dr. Colman came in, her eyes glued to my chart.

"Hey, E.J., I hear you're not feeling too well," she said, smiling and grabbing my foot to wiggle. "Home pregnancy test said positive, right?"

"Yes," I said.

"Your blood pressure is elevated. According to your records, it's usually so normal as to be disgusting."

"I try," I said.

Dr. Colman put down the chart and sat down on the stool next to me. "We need to do a quick ultrasound on you, okay?"

"This early?" I asked.

"It's all part of the diagnostic," she said.

I nodded. What did I know? I hadn't been pregnant in nine years. Things change.

After another quick barf-stop at the bathroom, Willis and I met Dr. Colman in her office. Her smile wasn't as bright as usual. She showed Willis and me to chairs, and said, "Well, you're not exactly pregnant."

Willis and I looked at each other. "What does that mean?" I finally asked.

"You have a condition called molar pregnancy, or trophoblastic tumor," she said. "Basically, it's a rare type of growth that occurs during pregnancy and grows in the placenta, and it prevents the fertilized egg from developing. It looks like a tiny cluster of white grapes. The first clues were your hypertension, nausea, and vomiting, and when I examined you I noticed your uterus was too large for dates." At our looks of confusion, she said, "Your EDC— estimated date of confinement—is calculated on your LMP—last menstrual period—and the gestational age of the fetus by ultrasound. Your uterus was too big for what should be the gestational age. The ultrasound confirmed it."

"Tumor?" I said. It seemed to be the only word I'd heard in all she'd said. Tumor.

"Eighty percent of these moles are benign," Dr. Colman said. "If, however, this one isn't, it means hysterectomy and maybe some chemotherapy. This is a very curable cancer."

Cancer. She said the "C" word. I felt as if I were going to vomit again, and I didn't think it had anything to do with my condition. My condition—cancer. Cancer.

I felt Willis's hand grabbing for mine; he squeezed my fingers, and if he hadn't been such a big boy, I might have broken his with my return squeeze.

"So what's the next step?" Willis asked. He had to; my voice was gone, along with most of my reasoning.

"First we do a D&C. One of the major symptoms of this is a high HCG hormone level. After the D&C, the level should go down. That's the first indicator that the mole is benign. If it doesn't go down, we wait three weeks, keep an eye on the HCG levels, and test again. Like I said, these things statistically are eighty percent benign, so the level should go down right away."

"And if it doesn't?" I found myself asking.

"Then we remove your uterus and start you on chemotherapy."

Dr. Colman grabbed her calendar and said, "Okay, how about a week from tomorrow? Next Tuesday. That sound good to you?"

"For the D&C?" Willis asked.

Dr. Colman nodded.

"That's fine," Willis said. "Right, honey, that's fine?"

I nodded. "A week from this Tuesday," I repeated.

We drove home, with me thinking, *A week and a day before I find out if I have cancer.* That also meant a week and a day that I didn't have cancer—

if the answer was bad. Or a week and a day that I did have cancer, if the answer was good.

Strange how the mind works.

I could die. I'd never thought about it before. I was thirty-nine years old and I could die.

Then I thought about the baby I'd thought I was having. Would I grieve that baby? Probably not. It hadn't been with me long enough to feel it, to know it. It had never really been a baby, just an egg that turned into nasty little white grapes.

Well, I thought, the good news was I wasn't pregnant; the bad news was . . . too awful to contemplate.

I've never really tried to hide anything from my children—except maybe sex. I mean, I've always been open about my moods—sad, mad, glad, whatever. They knew when we had financial troubles, knew when we were flush. They knew who I liked and who I didn't, even though they probably shouldn't know that.

I've never been big on subterfuge, even when it was the right thing to do. Maybe that's why Graham and I have had trouble over the years, with his thinking himself my equal in maturity and intelligence. Which I sometimes think is the truth, even though our family therapist says I need to stop that kind of thinking.

But this I had to hide. This "C" word I had to hide.

I woke up Tuesday morning thinking about it. Just like I'd gone to sleep the night before thinking about it. That I hadn't dreamt of it was surprising—or maybe I had and just suppressed whatever dreams this new knowledge had inspired.

Willis was bleary-eyed and carrying matched monogrammed luggage under his eyes. I took it he hadn't slept well the night before.

"Promise me you'll remarry," I said, before either of us had gotten out of bed.

Willis raised his arm, palm outward. "Don't *even* go there!" he said.

"I mean it," I said. "Promise you'll remarry."

"No, I won't promise that! Why should I? Are you insinuating I wouldn't make a good single parent? Don't you think I can make the kids happier with just me as their parent than marrying somebody just to have a warm body in the house to cook and clean?"

"Okay," I said. "Promise me you *won't* remarry."

He laughed. I laughed. And then we held each other long enough to make everybody late to work and school.

But it was worth it.

Around noon the phone rang. I answered on the second ring.

"Hello?"

"E.J.? This is Arlene Whitby, Michael's mother," the voice on the other end said.

All my personal problems had wiped the Whitbys' existence from my mind. "Oh, Arlene, hi, how are you?"

"Fine," she said, her voice edgy. "You men-

tioned Michael and your daughter playing together—''

''Over here,'' I said quickly—way too quickly.

''Of course,'' she said, ''at your house. I was
wondering if today would be okay. I have a dentist
appointment and I couldn't make it for any time
other than three o'clock, and the kids get out at two-
thirty—''

''How about if I just pick Michael up from school
with my kids, then you can pick him up whenever
you want?''

''That would be great. I really appreciate it. I'll
call the school and let them know you'll be picking
him up.''

''Okay, great. Then I'll see you later this
afternoon.''

''Yes. And, E.J.—''

''Yes?''

''Thank you,'' she said and hung up.

There was so much emotion in that ''thank you''
I felt ashamed for having said ''over here'' so em-
phatically. But only for a moment.

The teacher had been notified and I got all the
kids—my three, Luna's two, and Arlene's one—into
the minivan and headed home. Michael was entertaining the girls, and, although the older boys had
looked at the child askance at first—being aware of
who he was and probably fully cognizant of his father's crimes—they soon ignored him and the girls
as older children will younger. They were too insig-
nificant to pay much attention to.

The afternoon went the way of most afternoons—
fights about homework, what was considered a

proper after-school snack, and whether or not playing three hours of Nintendo constituted a learning experience.

By 6 P.M. I was thinking of calling Arlene to find out what was keeping her, when Willis's car pulled in the driveway. He lovingly tucked the Ghia into the garage, rubbing a dirt spot off with the sleeve of his shirt, and sauntered into the family room.

"Hey, gorgeous," he said, kissing me. Then he spied the extra child. "Who's this?" he asked smiling.

Megan jumped up from the cartoon show the three were watching. "Daddy, this is my friend Michael. Michael, this is my daddy!"

Michael stood up and held out his hand like a little gentleman. Willis shook it solemnly. "Nice to meet you, Michael," he said, then pulled me into the living room.

"Michael?" he asked, one eyebrow raised.

"As in Whitby, Jr.," I said.

"Good God, E.J.!"

"He's a child, Willis, and if you say one more word I swear I'm going to—"

I wasn't able to finish my threat because the doorbell rang. *Thank God,* I thought, *Arlene's finally here.*

"There's his mother," I said to Willis. "So just shut up!"

I walked to the door and opened it.

It wasn't Arlene Whitby but Abby Dane standing there. "E.J.," she said, smiling. "Marsha Rayburn asked me to bring this to you. It's the list of acceptable treats she wants brought to the class party next week.''

She handed me a sheet of paper filled with words like ''celery,'' ''wheat germ,'' and ''bran.''

''Oh, the kids are gonna love this,'' I said.

Abby rolled her eyes. ''You know Marsha. If it tastes good it must be bad for you.''

I heard something behind Abby and looked up. To my horror, Michael Whitby, Sr., was coming up the walk to my front door.

I just stared at him. My usual witty rejoinders seemed to have totally dried up.

''I'm here to pick up Michael,'' he said. He didn't smile.

Abby Dane whirled around, staring bug-eyed and open-mouthed at Whitby.

''What are you doing here?'' she demanded.

He glared at her, then looked at me. ''My son,'' he said.

I felt a hand on my arm and was moved aside.

''What are *you* doing here?'' Willis said, his face red, his hands shaking.

''I came to pick up my son,'' Whitby said, face matching Willis's in color, fists beginning to clinch.

I moved myself in front of Willis. ''Mr. Whitby, your son is welcome here,'' I said. ''Anytime. But I would prefer that his mother pick him up.''

''He's my kid, lady, and I'll do whatever I feel like doing, got that?''

Abby straightened up to her full five-feet-four. ''You should just leave! And I don't just mean the Pughs' house, mister! I mean the community! Hell, the state! While you're at it—''

Whitby smiled at Abby. "You have a little girl, don't you? I saw her with you at the school. Blonde?"

Abby doubled over as if Whitby had physically hit her. She ran around him, down the walk to her car.

"You asshole," I said to Whitby.

"Go get the kid," Willis said, shoving me slightly away from the menace at the front door.

I went into the family room.

"Michael, your dad's here to pick you up," I said.

Michael jumped up, his face flushing. "My dad?" he asked.

"Come on, honey," I said, taking his hand.

The girls started to get up, too.

"No!" I said, too quickly and too loudly. Trying to calm my voice I said, "Say goodbye to Michael now, girls. He has to go."

They did as they were told and I walked the boy to the door. He said a quiet "thank you" under his breath, but didn't look at me when he left. The look his father gave me was more than enough.

Michael Whitby
Journal Entry—October 29

I'm so angry my hands are shaking. I almost raised my hand to Arlene, that's how mad I am! When I got home from work, Arlene was just pulling in the driveway. Supper hadn't even been started. I know some husbands would be angry about that fact alone, but I try not to be that kind of husband. What got me was Mikey wasn't with her. When I asked where he was, she got all defensive, which got my back up.

I know Arlene. She gets defensive whenever she does something wrong, so I was getting worried even before I got her to tell me where she'd taken my son! Come to find out she'd left him at the home of the man who was causing all the trouble at my house! Him and his fat wife!

I tried to calm myself down. I told her I'd go pick him up, and Arlene started getting all fidgety again, saying no she'd do it. Well, I just looked at her. Telling me no? Who does she think she is?

So I went calmly to the house of those people where Arlene had left my son, and the man started in on me as soon as he opened the door! Like I didn't have a right to pick up my own child!

God forgive me, but I wanted to strike out! I wanted to hit him and his fat wife and Arlene and anybody else that got in my way! Including the skinny woman who was giving me lip! Well, I guess I showed her! I almost laughed, the way she was so afraid of me! That's how angry I was! Lord only knows what those people were filling Mikey's ears with—the boy would barely talk to me all the way home. And then when we got home, he ran to his mother like I'm some sort of ogre! I think three years alone with Arlene has had a negative influence on my son. It scares me to see him behaving like that. I need to get him away from Arlene for a while—maybe take him camping, something like that. Lord, I'm just so frustrated!

I think I'll call Mandy. She'll help me calm down.

"Willis, I'm sorry," I said later that evening. The kids were in bed and we were alone in the family room, TV muted through a commercial.

"Sorry about what?" my husband said lightly. Way too lightly.

"You know for what. I had no idea that man would show up here. I should have thought it through—"

Willis patted my hand. "It's okay, honey. Don't worry about it. I'll take care of it." He kissed me gently on the cheek. "Really, it's okay."

I looked at my husband and light dawned. "You don't want to upset me, right?" I said. "You're mad as all get out about this, but you're stuffing it because you don't want to upset me because you think I have cancer!"

"I do not think you have cancer! I just don't see any reason to yell about this!" Willis yelled at me.

"Since when?" I yelled back. "You've done nothing but yell about this from day one!"

"I'm trying to be reasonable!"

"Why? Because you think I have cancer! That's why!" I said. I burst into tears and ran to the bedroom, slamming the door and locking it behind me.

Well, hormones will be hormones, I suppose.

Willis used a screwdriver to get into the bedroom some time later. I feigned sleep as he crawled quietly in beside me.

"I'm sorry," I finally said.

He reached for my hand. "Me, too."

I moved toward him, putting my head in the crook of his armpit. "I'm scared," I said.

"Me, too," he said again. He put his finger under my chin and lifted my face so he could see it. "But Dr. Colman said, worse-case scenario, if this *is* cancer, it's very, very curable."

"I think she said only one very," I corrected.

"Let me keep my illusions," he said.

"Okay, very, very."

"The point is, babe," he said, settling down and snuggling up to me, "eighty percent of these things are benign, right? And you've got to admit, you and I usually go with the percentages. I mean, we've got a house in the suburbs, two-point-three children—"

"Don't let Graham hear you say that—"

"Christ, we even have a minivan. Honey, we go with the norm. And norm in this case is benign, right?"

"Because we have a minivan I'm going to be all right?" I asked skeptically.

"Exactly," Willis said.

Strangely enough, I had a good night's sleep after that.

Rene Tillery called me the next day. "Are you out of your mind?" she said by way of greeting.

"Probably. Who is this?" I asked.

"Don't be an idiot, E.J. It's Rene. Abby Dane called me last night and said she saw *him* at your house!"

"Who?" I asked. "Willis? Graham? The Orkin man?"

"You know, I always did think you had a strange sense of humor, E.J. Now I know it's because you are just sick! Really sick!"

I sighed. "What is it you want, Rene?"

"What was that man doing at your house? Have you totally lost your mind?"

"Rene, if I want to invite the devil himself to my house, I can't see where it's any of your business," I said.

"Well, you can just tell your husband we don't need him at the vigils anymore! I won't have this kind of behavior contaminating my campaign!"

"If you don't want Willis there, Rene, I suggest you tell him."

I hung up.

Rene had a way about her, that was for sure. Personally, I was totally sick about the fact that Michael Whitby, Sr., had shown up on my front porch. The thought of that man anywhere near my children made my bowels ache.

I'd been doing what I thought was the right thing. I'd invited a child over to play. It should have worked. Arlene Whitby should have picked up her son. Michael, Sr., should never have gotten near my home and family.

But he did. That was that. He did. I'd made a gesture and been slapped in the face for it.

I didn't like Rene Tillery, but she was right.

I didn't like what the community was doing, but they were right.

I hated the idea of ostracizing any child, but now maybe I would.

I popped one of the pills Dr. Colman had given me to keep from vomiting.

Seven

Halloween was fast approaching and the kids were making their yearly demands.

"I want to be a fairy princess," Megan said. "A blond fairy princess!"

"I want to go as a ballerina! I can use my ballet stuff from last summer, huh, Mama?" Bessie said.

"I'm not dressing up," Graham said. "That's for babies. Although I will need a dozen eggs and a couple of bars of soap."

"I'm supposed to supply you with the means to commit vandalism?" I asked my son, an eyebrow raised.

"That's not vandalism," Graham countered. "It's just good, clean fun."

"Shall we ask Luna the official county position on that?" I asked.

Graham rolled his eyes and headed for the stairs. "You know, you're getting pretty conservative in your old age, Ma."

I called Vera, my mother-in-law, to get her opinion on a blond princess costume. Okay, that's not exactly true. I called Vera because she sews and I don't and I figured if I asked for her opinion she'd volunteer to make the costume. Hey, manipulation is an art form.

"Well, I got some stuff left over from that prom dress I made for Brenna last spring," she said, mentioning her ward and my friend, Brenna McGraw, now a sophomore at Northwestern in Illinois. "And a little stuff left from the wedding veil I helped Erma make for her granddaughter. I think I can piece something together. Now, as far as the blond wig is concerned, honey, you are on your own."

"Personally, I'm not sure what's wrong with being a redheaded princess," I said.

"Sometimes everybody wants to be just a little different from what they are," Vera said. "Specially when what they are is as noticeable as you and your children."

"Are you saying I'm obnoxiously redheaded?" I asked.

"You said that, I didn't. Bring Megan around tomorrow after school so I can take some measurements," Vera said, and rang off.

I hung up the phone, trying not to think that tomorrow was Thursday, which would mean four more days of not knowing if I had cancer. I tried not to think about it at all, but it was like trying not to think about the elephant in the living room. Kind of hard to do.

I'm sure there have been times in my life when I've been more depressed—like shortly after the deaths of Bessie's birth parents. Those were hard times. Those were worse times than now, I told myself.

Or maybe not. That was straightforward grief and anger. The deed had been done. My friends were dead and I was left to pick up the pieces.

This was different. This was a waiting game. Not only was I waiting to find out if I was going to live or die, there was also the Michael Whitby waiting game. Would he strike again? Or more to the point, *when* would he strike again? And in dying, would I leave my daughters more vulnerable to the Michael Whitbys of this world?

I couldn't die, I decided. I just didn't have time for that. I had way too much to do to be packing it in now. I had kids to raise, books to write, a husband to terrorize and make love to. Willis would never find a woman who fit him like I did. That was a given. And no one could love my kids the way I did. Okay, maybe Willis could find someone who liked to bake and knew how to sew, but we had his mother for that.

I decided I could not be replaced. Therefore, the tumor would be benign, just like eighty percent of these cases were. And if it wasn't, well, as Willis said, it was a very, very, very curable cancer. Okay, maybe he only said two very's, and Marta Colman only said one, but this was my life we were talking about and my decision. And my decision was that this was going to be a very, very, very curable cancer. And I was strong enough to fight it.

The good news was maybe I'd lose a few pounds.

The next day I dropped the kids off at Vera's for Megan's fitting and drove to the Codderville Library. It was spitting rain when I left Vera's; this, however, turned into a deluge as I parked in the library's parking lot. I looked in vain for the umbrella I usually kept in the van, finally remembering I'd taken it in the house the last time it had rained.

I got out and ran for the library entrance, jumping over puddles and shielding my head from the rain with my purse. It did very little good.

In the library's medical section I found a little bit of information on my diagnosis: trophoblastic disease. The first definition said, "A hydatidiform mole is the end stage of a degenerating pregnancy in which the villi have become hydropic and the trophoblastic elements have proliferated. Persistent trophoblastic disease is a local invasion of the myometrium by the villi of the hydatidiform mole."

I read it four times and still had no idea what it said.

I went to the librarian and asked for a medical dictionary and looked up the words I didn't know. Which was most of them. A hydatidiform mole was a "fleshy mass or tumor" (that word again), "formed in the uterus by a degeneration or abortive development of an ovum." Okay, that made some kind of sense.

What was villi? The plural of villus. Great. What was villus? "A small vascular process or protrusion, especially such a protrusion from the free surface of a membrane.'' A bump. Okay, the villi—or bump—became hydropic. What's hydropic? ''Pertaining to or affected with dropsy.'' Great. I thought dropsy was something older women had in books about the Victorians. Like swooning. No such luck. Dropsy was ''the abnormal accumulation of serous fluid in the cellular tissue or in a body cavity.'' Now I was becoming totally confused. ''Serous fluid''—''pertaining to or resembling serum or producing or containing serum, as serous gland or cyst.''

Okay, I reasoned. *The bumps—villi—got filled with an abnormal amount of serum fluid, which formed a fleshy mass or tumor in the uterus.* I was beginning to see some light. Not terribly bright light—a kind of gray, dull light—but light nonetheless.

''Persistent trophoblastic disease is a local invasion of the myometrium by the villi of the hydatidiform mole.''

Myometrium? ''The smooth muscle coat of the uterus which forms the main mass of the organ.''

Okay, the muscle coat of my uterus has been invaded by the bumps of a fleshy mass. Now, that pulled it all down to size. I still wasn't sure what it meant, but getting some of the words out of the way, translating it into English, helped.

I spent a good hour at the library, reading everything I could find on the subject and then translating that into English. The two things I discovered without having to translate were that a mole is more common in older patients (I was thirty-nine, for God's sake! That's not old!), and ten times more

Asian women got the disease than non-Asian. Which meant that somewhere in the Orient, ten women were getting the same bad news I had just gotten. Misery may love company, but even I wasn't selfish enough to wish this on anyone else.

I drove back to Vera's with the feeling that I had a handle on the whole thing. If I knew what it was, could understand it, then I could fight it.

The deluge at the library had calmed down to a mere drip by the time I reached Vera's, but it was still too wet to send the kids outside. Instead I suggested they go in Brenna's old room and see what they could do about rearranging her drawers. Even Graham went for that; he's had a crush on Brenna since the day he met her and going through her things would be just up his alley. I know, I know, I've been spouting off for weeks about the right to privacy, but in this case I wasn't terribly worried. Now well into her second year at Northwestern, there was very little of a personal nature left in Brenna's room.

Once the kids were out of our hair, I admired the work Vera had already started on the fairy princess dress. The woman is a whiz when it comes to needle and thread.

It was then that I sat her down in the kitchen and told her what the doctor had discovered.

Halfway through my explanation she began mopping the kitchen floor.

I put my hand on hers as she passed. "Vera, it's okay. It really is. This is a very curable cancer. If it even is cancer. There's an eighty-percent chance the tumor will be benign."

She looked at me. "What do you want me to do?"

"Can you keep the kids Monday night? Willis and I have to be in early for the D&C Tuesday morning—"

"And I'll keep 'em Tuesday night, too—"

"I should be fine—"

"Let's just plan on me keeping 'em. That way you and Willis can celebrate the good news." She smiled at me.

I smiled back. "Good idea," I said, knowing I could have done a lot worse in the mother-in-law department.

I decided not to call my mother or otherwise alert the media until there was either something or nothing to tell. My mother doesn't handle adversity well and the waiting could put her in bed with a cold compress until next Tuesday.

It seemed to be raining a great deal harder on our side of the Colorado River, and once we got in the house I had to get started finding buckets for the two leaks in the new construction—one in the family room and one in the master bath around the skylight—that seemed to be a permanent part of the new decor.

With Halloween coming up on Saturday, I had too much to think about to wallow more than every ten minutes or so in my misery. There was so much I didn't want to think about; like my condition and Michael Whitby. But thinking about Whitby was preferable to thinking about my condition.

I knew in a lot of ways I had been wrong—although deep in my heart of hearts, I knew I had been right about some things. Michael Whitby did have the right to live where he chose. Once we start fencing off areas where certain people had to live, how far away from complete fascism were we? The man had served his time. It wasn't enough time, I'll admit. And that needed to be addressed. People—men and women both—sexually and physically abused and even killed children and received unbelievably light sentences. Especially if the children they abuse are their own.

Unfortunately, children don't vote. But parents do—or should. Black Cat Ridge would have been saved the moral dilemma we were now in if Michael Whitby had received a sentence befitting his crime—ten to twenty years at least—and if he had served a greater portion of it. How can a man whose crime is abusing children be considered to have been on good behavior when there were no children around to tempt him? It made no sense.

Until there are laws to protect children and punishments that match the crimes, our country will always have the moral dilemma of what to do with these people when they've served their time. Communities will continue to yell "Not in my backyard," and have the right to that feeling. Yet the Michael Whitbys of this world have rights, too. They are human beings—although some may argue that point—and this is supposedly still a free country—although, again, an arguable point.

This is a dilemma that a Texas housewife/romance writer with a B.A. in English lit is not totally equipped to handle. But it's not black or white. It can't be. It's not "not in my backyard," because, if not mine, then whose?

I picked up the phone and called Arlene Whitby. She answered on the second ring.

"Would it be okay if Michael went trick or treating with Megan and Bessie Saturday night?" I asked.

There was a long silence. Finally she said, "Yes. It would definitely be okay. What time should I drop him off?" she asked.

We made the arrangements and I hung up. This was something I'd have to try to explain to Willis, but it wasn't something I had to explain to myself. I could deal with it.

Willis came home Thursday evening, wet and in a lather that had little to do with the weather. "Guess who called me today?" he said, his teeth clenched.

I shrugged. I was in the kitchen, cutting up vegetables and not particularly interested.

"Rene Tillery," he said.

I stopped what I was doing and turned to face him, leaning against the sink. Inwardly I grinned. I almost felt sorry for Rene—almost. "Oh? What did she have to say?"

"She tried to fire me," Willis said.

"Fire you?" I asked innocently.

"Yeah. Said she didn't need me on the vigils anymore. Because that asshole Whitby showed up at our house we were obviously sicko-perverts ourselves and she didn't want me—or you, by the way—involved in her righteous group."

I couldn't hold the grin back. "What did you tell her?" I asked.

"Would you like me to leave out the obscenities?" he asked.

I nodded.

"Basically, I told her it was a free country and I could make my own picket signs and that I would be at Whitby's house when and if I felt like marching wherever I felt like it and she could go . . . jump up a rope. So to speak."

"And what did she say?" I asked.

"Not much," Willis said, grinning back at me. "She sputtered though."

"Sputtered?"

"Yeah. It was cool," he grinned and moved toward me, putting his arms around my waist and drawing me close. With a comical face, he tried for an imitation of Rene Tillery sputtering.

I laughed. "You can't do it justice without a ponytail," I said.

"I would like to have seen her at that," he said. "What's for dinner?"

"Vegetarian lasagna," I said.

Willis made a face. "Does it have any meat in it?" he asked.

I rolled my eyes. "Of course," I said. "Most vegetarian dishes have loads of meat."

"Just checking," he said. "You never know."

"You going to picket tonight?"

"Is the Pope Polish?"

"Give Rene a big old smooch for me," I said.

*   *   *

The rain of the day before was the forerunner of a cold front. Friday dawned cold and damp. I had to finally bring out some of the winter clothes for the kids. It was definitely sweater under raincoat time.

"Mama, it's not gonna be like this tomorrow night, is it?" Megan whined.

"The weatherman said it should clear up this afternoon," I said.

"Cause I can't wear a sweater over my princess outfit, it'll look stupid. Did you get me a wig yet?"

"We'll go look for one this afternoon," I replied, trying to get her to hold her sweater sleeve while I helped her with her raincoat.

"It's gotta be blond," Megan said.

"Should look great with those freckles," Graham said, pinching his sister as he walked by.

"Hey, I'll knock your block off!" Megan screamed.

"Ooooo, I'm scared!" Graham yelled back, pretending to shudder.

"Mama!" Megan yelled at me.

"Stop squirming or I'll never get this raincoat on you," I said.

"Old Freckles can't even dress herself yet!" Graham taunted.

Megan pulled away from me, one sleeve of her raincoat flapping in the breeze behind her as she headed after her brother.

Bessie sat at the table and rolled her eyes. "Those two," she said with a shake of her head.

"Where's your raincoat?" I asked her.

She shrugged. "I think I threw it away."

"What?" I asked.

"Well, not really threw it away. I put it in that bag you took to the Goodwill box last summer."

I sat down at the kitchen table. "Why?" I demanded.

Bessie rolled her eyes again. "Gawd, Mother, it had the Little Mermaid on it! You don't expect me to wear something like that in the fourth grade, do you?"

Well, she had me there. I stood up and went to the hall closet and got her new jacket and an umbrella. "Take these," I said.

She nodded, finished her cereal, and went in search of her siblings.

I had to go into Codderville for office supplies, so Willis and I decided to meet at McDonald's for lunch. It had stopped raining, but the weather was still foul—low-hanging clouds and a cold damp wind out of the north. I could only hope the weatherman was right with his prediction of clear skies for Halloween—but predicting the weather in Texas is at best a futile proposition, and at worst just plain stupid.

Willis was already there when I arrived at the McDonald's and I parked next to his Ghia. Inside I found him at a booth with someone else. The other person's back was to me, so all I knew as I approached was that he was male. When I got to their table, Keith Tillery, the illustrious Rene's husband, stood to greet me.

"Hey, E.J.," he said, shaking my hand.

"Hi, Keith," I said, scooting into the booth next to my husband. "How are you?"

Keith grinned. "As well as can be expected while still married to my current wife," he said.

"Rene's doing what she thinks is best," I said, although even as I said it I knew how prissy it sounded.

Keith sighed. "Rene's got a good heart," he said. "And organizational skills to rival the U.N. She just gets very *excitable*."

"Well, Willis and I don't agree on this issue either," I said. "But I figure our marriage can weather it. It's weathered worse."

"Oh, I agree with Rene in principle," Keith said. "The guy's scum and shouldn't exist. On the other hand, I'm not big on government interference in personal matters. And any way you look at it, even on the local level, what Rene's doing is organized interference in someone's personal freedom. I mean, people should be able to live how they want to. Look at Ruby Ridge. Those people had every right in the world—"

"To be selling illegal firearms?" Willis asked.

"Man, read your constitution," Keith said. "Government interference in your personal freedom is against the constitution! Of course, so's taxation! You know what I paid in taxes last year?"

"What has this got to do with Michael Whitby?" I asked, not wanting to get into a tax discussion.

"It's an individual rights issue," Keith said. "I mean, to say the community has rights over the individual sounds pretty Marxist to me."

"Marxist?" I said, suddenly finding myself ready to fight for the other side. "The community—in the form of your wife, may I add—is trying to protect our children—''

"I protect *my* children!" Keith said, leaning across the table. "Willis protects *his* children! We don't need a goddamn committee to protect our children! If the world was thinking right, the fathers of the girls that asshole molested would have lynched Whitby back in East Texas and this would all be a moot point."

"You can't mean that!" I said.

"He's got a point," my husband said.

I glared at him.

"Lynching is hardly civilized!" I said.

"To hell with civilized!" Keith said. "You hurt mine, I hurt you! That's the way of the west. Hell, my granddaddy killed a man for shooting his dog and the judge let him go! Said if the asshole had shot his dog, he'da killed him too!"

"Oh, for God's sake," I said. "This is the nineteen-nineties, Keith. Try to focus!"

"Hey, E.J., I agree with you! What's the problem? I don't see any reason for all this boycotting and picketing and crap! Leave the guy be, is all I'm saying. And if he messes with me or mine, then that's the end of that!"

I shook my head. "Excuse me while I go get a Big Mac," I said, scooting out of the booth and hoping the conversation would go in another direction before I got back.

I stood in line waiting my turn while the children behind the counter looked at the pictures on the cash register and tried to figure out what to do. And I thought about what Keith had said.

I didn't know Keith well, although I was beginning to know him better. Strange that different ends of the political spectrum could end up in the same place—but for different reasons.

Luckily, by the time I got back with my Big Mac and Diet Coke, Keith was gone.

Willis looked at me and grinned. "Does it make you feel all warm and toasty to find someone who agrees with you?"

"Shut up," I said.

Michael Whitby
Journal Entry—October 30

I've had it with this place and their humanistic, liberal thinking! How liberal can these people be when they refuse to show forgiveness or kindness to others? This certainly isn't a Christian community, for all the churches they have scattered around! Sunday Christians, that's all they are!

I'm taking Mikey trick or treating tomorrow night and Black Cat Ridge can just lump it! They don't show my kid some respect, there's gonna be some bloody noses, and I'm not kidding around here!

Maybe Mandy will come with Mikey and me. That would be nice. The girl needs to get out, be with a normal family. And if Mikey's there, maybe she won't come on to me like she's been doing. It's hard on the resolve the way she acts when we're alone. Smiling at me, touching my hand, acting like I'm the king of the universe. She's got really great skin, soft and smooth. And that firm little butt she swings whenever she walks. Taunting me with it. But if Mi-

*key's there, it'll be okay. She can't come on to me
with Mikey there. And I know I can handle this. The
girl needs my guidance, that's all. The poor kid's
so alone it's enough to make a grown man cry.*

The sun rose on Halloween day, with a temperature in the low seventies and a cool breeze out of
the north. The rain of the past few days and the drop
in temperature had scoured the world clean, leaving
it smelling new and fresh and feeling crisp. It still
meant a sweater over the princess costume, but there
could have been worse disasters than that.

The grammar school was having their annual Halloween Fest starting at 6 P.M. and lasting until eight
that night. For the first time in recorded history, I
wasn't in charge of a booth.

Arlene Whitby was bringing Michael, Jr., to the
fest and he would join the girls for that and for trick
or treating afterwards. Willis was staying home to
man the fort and hand out candy, in a desperate
attempt to stave off the tricking by offering treats.
Graham and his pals had gone "to a party" somewhere. He wasn't telling, but I noticed my toilet
paper supply had dwindled.

The girls were totally decked out. Bessie was
wearing her ballerina costume from her summer ballet classes, complete with tutu, and Megan was wearing the midnight blue and white lace princess
concoction made by my mother-in-law. The white
Dynel wig was as blond as I could find.

Arlene and Michael, Jr., were waiting by her car
in the school parking lot when I pulled up in the
minivan.

The girls ran up to Michael, showing off their costumes. Michael was wearing a pirate costume and looked adorable. The three of them yelled bye to Arlene and me and headed for the school.

"Thanks for doing this, E.J.," Arlene said.

"My pleasure," I told her.

She looked off at the children running toward the grounds. "He wanted to come to this so badly, but I was afraid to bring him. You don't know how people react to me."

I followed her look and nodded my head. "I'm beginning to see that, Arlene, and I'm sorry." I looked at her. "None of this is your fault."

"They think it is. They think a decent woman wouldn't be married to a man who'd do that. Or if I'd been a better wife, he wouldn't have needed to do that. Or if I'd been a decent woman, I'd have left him." She sighed. "A million reasons why I'm as guilty as he is."

"I'm not sure I understand why you stayed, Arlene, but that's your call, not mine."

Still not looking at me, her voice low, Arlene said, "My daddy always said, you make your bed, you lie in it." She shook herself. "I'd better go. What time do you think you'll be getting Michael home?" she asked.

"Before ten for sure," I said.

She smiled. "Thanks again," she said, got in her car and left.

I walked through the wet grass toward the school grounds and the writhing, screaming throng of ghosties and goblins.

We played the games at every booth on the

schoolyard, and went through the "fun room," handling the peeled grape "eyes" and spaghetti "guts" that were offered up in the dark. We ate cotton candy, ducked for apples, and won cheap plastic toys.

It was as we were rounding the corner of the cafetorium that reality hit us all. Rene Tillery and her daughters were walking our direction. Rene saw us and stopped dead in her tracks. She stared at Michael, Jr., then looked at me.

She smiled. "I certainly see I have my next project cut out for me," she said.

"Excuse us, Rene," I said, trying to move the kids around her.

She stepped in front of me, blocking my way and definitely getting in my space. "As soon as I get the Whitbys out of Black Cat Ridge, I guess I'd better start on ridding the community of the Pughs."

If we'd been alone I'm afraid I would have slapped her. But the kids were there. It's amazing how you're forced to play grown up when your children are watching.

"I know a shrink in Codderville I'll recommend to you, Rene," I said, smiling as sweetly as she was. "I think you could use a little help."

I moved the children around her and headed toward the parking lot. Michael, Jr.'s head was bowed as he reached the car. I got the girls in the van and pulled Michael aside.

I knelt in front of him. "Honey, there are some stupid and mean people around here. Mrs. Tillery is one of them. I know I can't ask you to forget what she said, but you do need to remember who it came from: a stupid person. And there's really no reason to pay much attention to stupid people.''

He nodded his head, although he was still looking at the ground. I lifted his chin to look into his eyes, and smiled at him. ''Hey,'' I said, ''you're a pirate, right? Pirates don't have to listen to stupid people!''

He tried a tentative smile. ''Yeah,'' he said. The smiled turned to a grin. ''Argh!'' he said, baring his teeth.

I laughed. ''Exactly!'' I helped him into the van. ''Watch out, girls,'' I said, ''we've got a mean pirate getting in here!''

We headed out of the parking lot, now more excited about trick or treating than the fest. The moon was coming up, a full, round, yellow harvest moon, low in the sky and looking bigger than on any normal night. It was a real Halloween moon and the kids stared out the window at it, finding faces and shapes in the craters of the moon.

The girls each had a plastic jack-o-lantern with a backup pillowcase for any extra loot. Michael had a plastic grocery sack. I stayed in the car as they ran up to the houses, moving along slowly in their wake, being careful of the rug rats running the streets, and occasionally on the lookout for my very own juvenile delinquent, who remained hidden from my view.

We were nearing Friar Tuck Lane, the street the Whitbys lived on, when Megan came running back to the van ahead of the others. ''That lady won't open her door!'' she said, tears in her eyes. ''She's yelling at Michael!''

I turned off the engine and got out of the van. I recognized the house. Laura and Pate Wiley lived here. Pate owned a small oil field construction company. Willis had done work for him in the past and the four of us had gone out to dinner together a couple of times. Laura wasn't exactly my type, a little nervous, not interested in much more than her hair, nails, and skin, with an occasional thought to her children—daughters, whose hair, nails, and skin she worried about more than their brains. But I hadn't seen either of the Wileys at the meetings or vigils.

I walked up to the front door and knocked on it. Michael was standing on the sidewalk, looking at his feet again. The feisty pirate long gone.

"Laura," I called. "It's me, E.J. Open up."

The door opened against the chain.

"Is he gone?" she whispered.

"Who?" I asked.

"That horrible child! The one who hurts other children!"

"My God, Laura, what are you talking about?" I pointed behind me at my daughters and Michael, Jr. "He's nine years old, for Christ's sake! His father's the one who served time, not him! He's a child!"

Laura's eyes darted beyond me to the sidewalk where the children stood.

"Oh, God, he's coming!" Laura whispered and looked at me with fear in her eyes.

I looked behind me. Michael, Jr., was walking purposefully towards the Wileys' front door. "Is she like the one you were talking about, Mrs. Pugh? Just another stupid person?" he asked, his head held high.

I looked from him to Laura. "Yes, Michael. Just

another stupid person. And I bet she doesn't even give out good candy.''

I turned and took his hand and headed back to the van. I parked the van this time and walked up to the door with the kids. We hit a few more houses without incident and hauled in some incredible loot.

Ten o'clock came way too quickly for the kids— and not quite quickly enough for me. I bundled them in the minivan, admonishing them not to eat any of their candy until a grownup had gone through it, and headed for the Whitby house. I made the girls stay in the car as I walked Michael, Jr., up to the front door. There was a bale of hay sitting on the front porch with a full-sized rag doll sitting atop it. Instead of a face, the rag doll had a jack-o'-lantern for a head.

''Hey, that's cute,'' I said to Michael.

He laughed. ''Mama must have put that up after I left,'' he said. ''Neat, huh?''

And it was. Until I saw the bloody palm of the very humanlike hand of the rag doll.

Eight

I got Michael, Jr., away from the "rag doll" and into the house as quickly as I could.

Arlene met us in the foyer. "Is your husband home?" I asked her.

She shook her head. "No," she said.

I moved away from Michael, Jr., pulling Arlene with me. "Call 911 right now," I said, then went out the door and back to the minivan, where I got the girls and took them inside the house, shielding their sight of the "rag doll" with my body.

Arlene grabbed the girls and pulled them inside, then stepped out on the porch with me.

It was a large pumpkin, but even so the back had been smashed in, obviously so the pumpkin could be fitted easily around the human head underneath. The body and the pumpkin were both leaning against the side of Arlene's house, the one thing, I suppose, that kept it from toppling over.

"What is that?" she asked, looking at the full-sized "doll" on the bale of hay.

"Did you call the police?" I asked.

"Yes," she said, "but I didn't know what to tell them. Just asked that they get here right away. When I mentioned your name, there was some general consternation but—" She gasped. "My, God, E.J., there's blood—"

Arlene made a high-pitched sound, then covered her mouth as she backed into the door. "Oh, God, that's Michael's watch!" she said, pointing at the bloody arm.

Somehow, I was less than surprised to discover the body was probably that of Michael Whitby, Sr. Less than surprised, and more relieved than I'd care to admit.

Willis beat the police by about five minutes. Arlene stayed inside with the children, who were more than happy to continue playing in Michael, Jr.'s room, totally ignorant of what was going on outside, while Willis and I supervised the body.

"Maybe we should take off the pumpkin head," Willis suggested.

"You don't tamper with evidence, Willis. Luna would have your liver for lunch."

He bent down and peered in the eyeholes of the jack-o-lantern. "Looks like somebody's in there," he said.

"I know." I pointed to the back of the pumpkin head, leaning against the wall. "You can see the head there. And Arlene said that's her husband's watch."

"Shit," Willis said. "I suppose that's one way of handling the problem."

"Don't let the cops hear you," I said, as the sirens sounded coming up the street.

Two uniforms were the first on the scene. We showed them the "rag doll" and then moved away. From our vantage point in the front yard, however, we were able to see when the first cop took off the pumpkin head.

It was indeed the body of Michael Whitby, Sr., and there was what appeared to be a bullet hole in the center of his forehead.

The other uniform pulled us away and started asking questions. Who found the body? When did I find the body? Did we touch anything? Who's in the house? Did they touch anything? Could I identify the body? What was my relationship to the body? On and on and on. Finally, Willis suggested we go inside the house as the night was getting increasingly chilly.

Before we could go in, however, Elena Luna showed up. She gave me a look, then pulled the uniform who'd been talking to us over and they began a frantic whisper fest.

Finally, she left the uniform and walked over to Willis and me. "Jesus, Pugh," she said, looking at me, "why are you always around when these things happen?"

"I'm not!" I protested. "I'm rarely if ever around when these things happen!"

Luna raised an eyebrow and gave me a look. "The Lesters?" she said. "Brad McLemore?"

"This isn't my fault!" I said.

"I need to get my wife inside," Willis said, staring daggers at Luna. "It's cold out here."

"The kids inside?" Luna asked, her thumb pointing in the direction of the Whitby house.

I nodded. "I had to take the girls in when I found that thing. I don't think Michael, Jr., figured out what it was."

"Let's go," she said, leading the way to Arlene's front door. Arlene opened it as we got there, obviously having been watching the activity through the window.

"Is it—" she started.

I nodded my head and took her by the arm. Her knees seemed to buckle for an instant, then she straightened and walked with me slowly to the couch. She fell onto it and put her head in her hands.

"Oh, God, I wish I could cry," she said.

I put my arm around her shoulders. "You will," I said. "Maybe not right now, but you will."

She leaned back against the couch, resting her head on the back of it and closed her eyes.

"Who's going to mourn him?" she asked of no one.

"I need to know what went on here this evening, Mrs. Whitby," Luna said.

Arlene opened her eyes and tried to focus on the detective. "What do you mean?" she asked.

"Have you been home all evening?"

Arlene looked at me. "I took my son to the school

to meet Mrs. Pugh and her daughters around six.
Then I came home.''

"What time was that?''

Again Arlene looked at me. "I don't know. I
came straight home. I didn't stop at the store or
anything. Maybe six-fifteen at the latest. Maybe
six-ten.''

"Was your husband home then?'' Luna asked.

I took Arlene's hand and held it while she answered. "Yes,'' she said. "He'd come home while
I was gone.'' She gulped in air. "We had a fight.''

"About what?'' Luna asked.

Arlene glanced my way. "About me letting E.J.
take Mikey trick or treating. Michael wanted to do
that himself. Said he was planning on showing the
entire community.''

"Showing them what?'' Luna asked.

Arlene shrugged. "I don't know. I guess that they
couldn't bully him or intimidate him.''

Luna was taking copious notes. She wrote for a
minute and then looked up at Arlene. "Did he hit
you?'' she asked.

Arlene's shoulders straightened. "Michael never
hit me in our entire marriage,'' she said, pride in her
voice—maybe from finally finding something nice to
say about the man.

"Okay, you had words. Then what?''

Arlene shrugged. "He left. He usually did that
when he was mad about something.''

"What time would that have been?'' Luna asked,
pen poised.

Arlene looked at me, her face confused. "I don't
know,'' she said. "I really didn't look at a clock,

and the TV wasn't on. Maybe about fifteen minutes after I got home. Maybe half an hour. It couldn't have been longer than that.''

"So let's say somewhere between six-thirty and six-forty-five?"

Arlene nodded. "I guess," she said.

"Did he say where he was going?"

Arlene shook her head. "He never told me that. He'd just leave. He'd be gone for hours sometimes. I never knew where he was."

"Did you hear anything outside?" Luna asked.

Arlene shook her head. "No, I had my music on. I never heard a thing."

"Any kids ring the doorbell?"

Arlene laughed bitterly. "At this house? Would you let your children trick or treat here?"

Luna ignored the question. "So, Mrs. Whitby, what you're telling me is that you and your husband had a verbal disagreement, he slammed out of the house, and several hours later his dead body shows up on your front porch and you never heard a thing."

Arlene squeezed my fingers, looking at me with panic in her eyes. "I swear that's the truth, Detective! Why would I kill my husband?"

"Wives kill their husbands all the time, Mrs. Whitby, and vice versa. And with your husband's reputation, I wouldn't be surprised if you'd *want* to kill him."

Arlene squared her shoulders. "I wouldn't even divorce him, Detective, much less kill him. He's my son's father."

There was a knock at the door and Luna went to

it and conferred for a moment with the officer on the porch. She came back to where Arlene and I sat on the couch.

"They're taking the body away now, Mrs. Whitby. Would you like to see it before they go?"

Arlene nodded and stood up. I stood up with her, but she patted my hand. "Wait here, E.J. Thank you, but I have to do this on my own."

I could see Arlene and Luna through the front window as they walked up to the gurney. One of the attendants unzipped the plastic body bag and Arlene touched her husband's face. She nodded at Luna and came back inside.

"Why don't you and Mikey come home with the girls and me?" I suggested. "You can't stay here—" I started, but Arlene was already shaking her head.

"Thank you, E.J., that's very kind, but this is our home. I'm not going to let them run me out of my home. Out of Mikey's home."

I hugged her, her slight frame fragile and shaky from the night's encounter, then went to Mikey's room to get the girls.

This was one of those bad news/good news situations. The bad news was someone had murdered Michael Whitby; the good news was someone had murdered Michael Whitby.

I don't condone murder. In any way, shape, or form. No one should take another's life. That's God's provenance—not man's. On the other hand . . .

Sorry, I don't mean to sound cavalier. But Arlene Whitby was right: Who was going to mourn him?

NOT IN MY BACKYARD

His son, maybe. Although in some ways, even the child was going to be relieved of his burden.

Black Cat Ridge could get back to normal; no more vigils, no more picketing, no more frantic phone calls from parent to parent. Our children were once again safe from, if not all, at least one child molester.

But it was just too easy. It wasn't right to settle the moral dilemma this way. The issue was too pertinent, too "in our faces" to be resolved so simply.

A great weight had been lifted from the community, but it could come back. Any time. From any place. What happens the next time a released felon moves into the community? Do we just kill him, too?

Half of me was relieved, the half that was Mother. The half that was a rational, thinking adult wanted answers. Murder was no way to deal with the Michael Whitbys of this world. Who could set themselves up as judge and jury over another human being? And how did the taking of this life make the taker any higher on the evolutionary scale than Michael Whitby himself?

I'd worried myself silly before when I'd been involved in someone's death. Too many times I'd been the discoverer of a dead body—those of friends and enemies. Too many times someone I cared about had been accused of causing another's death.

Because of that I'd gotten myself involved— against the wishes of almost everyone in the world, including and especially my husband and homicide detective Elena Luna, my next-door neighbor—but what was my excuse for involvement this time? The fact that no one, not even the police, would give much of a big damn who killed Michael Whitby? That was certainly one reason.

One of the first things I've always asked myself when getting involved in something like this was: Who would benefit from the deceased's death? In Michael Whitby's case, however, the question should be: Who *wouldn't* benefit from his death? I couldn't think of a single person.

Who stood to gain? Maybe there was some insurance money, but probably not much. Whitby had just started his job with the city parks department; his insurance had probably not even kicked in yet. Maybe Arlene had a separate policy on him. If so, why would she kill him and leave him on her own front porch?

For exactly that reason, I told myself. Who would suspect a wife of doing something as stupid as that?

But Arlene Whitby didn't seem the devious sort. Of course, who really knows what's in another person's heart or head? But still, somehow, I didn't see her in the role of husband killer. It would have been simpler to just divorce him. No judge in his right mind would give a convicted child molester custody of a child, so she'd have no real custody battle.

Money? It all came back to that. A wife kills for love or money. Hell, most people kill for love or money. In Arlene's case, she already knew what Whitby was, that he wasn't exactly a faithful husband. Why kill him now in a fit of passion? Because she discovered he was up to his old tricks again?

I shuddered. The thought of Michael Whitby playing his games with another young girl made me sick to my stomach.

That left money. I needed to ask Luna about Whitby's insurance.

Not that she'd tell me, of course.

But that exercise in futility would keep my mind off Tuesday, and that was becoming my new mantra.

Sunday afternoon the doorbell rang. I was closest so I went to answer it. Arlene Whitby and Michael, Jr., stood on the porch, the rain behind them coming down in buckets.

I opened the door wide. "Y'all come in! You're soaked!" I took them both back to the laundry closet where there were some clean towels and helped them dry off. The girls, of course, were ecstatic to see Michael, Jr., ecstatic enough to share some of their loot from the night before.

Once fairly dry, Arlene nodded towards the living room and the two of us went in there.

"I got a call this morning from the security guard at Michael's office," she said. "He said Michael's car was there and needed to be moved."

"Did you call the police?" I asked.

Arlene shook her head. "No. I will, but I haven't yet. I just went there thinking—" She shook her head again. "I don't know what I was thinking, to tell the truth." She sighed. "But I found this."

She handed me an eight-and-a-half-by-eleven leatherbound book. Opening it, I saw written across the front page, "Journal—Michael Whitby—Private!!"

"Did you read it?" I asked her.

She nodded her head miserably. "Yes. Now you."

I sat back and read the journal entries. I was surprised and a little pissed off to see a mention of Willis and me in the pages, especially the part where he called me fat—twice—but I was totally sickened by the mention of a fifteen-year-old McDonald's employee named Mandy.

Michael Whitby had definitely been up to his old tricks. And the next victim was going to be—or already was—a fifteen-year-old named Mandy.

The last entry was dated October 31, the night he died.

Michael Whitby
Journal Entry—October 31

Arlene's gonna have to die. That's all there is to it. Every time I look at her I want to puke! And she's trying to take my son away from me! It's so obvious! She's so stupid thinking I don't know what she's up to! Well, I'm going to show her!

I need Mandy. Mandy will help me calm down. I'll get Mandy and together we'll find where Arlene has hidden Mikey, and then we'll go trick or treating just like I planned. And when Arlene is dead, Mandy can come live with Mikey and me, and I'll take care of them both. Mandy needs a strong male influence in her life. And that's what I'll be. And if something happens between us, well, then that's all in God's plan, isn't it?

I read the last entry and closed the book.

"If I show this to the police, they'll just have another reason to think I killed him," Arlene said. "Because they'll think I knew he was going to try to kill me." She burst into tears. "Oh, God, *now* I cry!" she said through her sobs.

"There's no way we can't show this to them," I told her.

"I know, I know," she sobbed. "But he did it again, E.J.! My God, he did it again!"

"Maybe not," I said. "Wouldn't he have mentioned it if there had been something going on between them?"

"I don't know," she said, looking up at me and sniffing, trying to get her crying under control. She shook her head. "God, he was so mean! Saying I didn't give him what he needed! What was that?" she asked me. "He never said what he needed! I never refused him! Ever! God's law is a wife lies down with her husband, and I did that! I did everything he asked of me! What more did he want?"

I put my arm around her. "Arlene, he was sick. It had nothing to do with you—"

She jumped up. "It had everything to do with me!" she shouted. "Didn't you read that filth? Didn't you see what he said? I failed him, E.J.! He did all those terrible things because I failed him in some way! And he was going to go on doing it because I couldn't fix it!"

I stood up and pushed her gently back down to the couch. "Shut up, Arlene," I said softly. "You don't want Mikey to hear this, right?"

She nodded and hung her head. "Oh, God, I'm just making everything worse!"

"I didn't realize you had such a large ego," I said, sitting down next to her and touching her hand.

She snapped her head up. "What?"

"Are you the center of the universe?" I asked.

Arlene gulped. "Why are you saying these things to me?"

"Because you'd have to think you were pretty damned important for all this to be your fault. I didn't realize you totally controlled your husband. That your word and deed was law in that house."

"No! My husband was head of our household! That's what my church teaches!"

"Then how could you control what Michael did or didn't do? How can you be responsible for his actions?"

Arlene leaned her head against the back of the couch and closed her eyes. "You're confusing me," she said, her voice barely above a whisper.

"We don't control other people, Arlene," I said. "We each have our own will—our own *God-given* will," I added for good measure, "and we make our own decisions. Michael made his. It wouldn't have mattered what you did or didn't do, Arlene, Michael was who he was and he did what he wanted to do."

"I failed him," she whispered.

"No, Arlene, he failed you. And Mikey. And everybody else. He's the one who did the bad things, not you. He's the one who ruined your family, not you. He's the one, Arlene. He failed, not you."

Arlene shook her head. "I could have done something!"

I turned to face her. "Tell you what," I said, "you tell me in so many words exactly what you could have done to stop Michael, and I'll agree with you. But not until you can do that."

She shook her head again. "You're turning everything upside down," she said.

"Because you were thinking while standing on your head," I said with a smile. "Now you're on your feet. Think about it from this angle."

"My mother said I chose Michael and I had to stay with him and bear the burden—"

"You didn't know who Michael really was when you chose him, Arlene."

"My pastor said that a good wife stood by her man no matter what, and that she had to take on his burdens like her own—"

"You did that. You stood by him. And you tried to take on his burdens, but how could you when you didn't even know what they were? Now he's dead, Arlene. Your job is over."

Arlene started to cry. She put her head against my chest and bawled, soaking my top with her tears.

I patted her back and let her go.

Before she left, I asked Arlene if I could borrow Michael's journal for a few minutes, telling her I'd bring it by her house in less than an hour. I left Willis with the kids and hightailed it to the mail store in the same shopping center as the Food Giant. There I used their copier to make my own copy of the journal, then drove it quickly by Arlene's house, telling her to go ahead and turn it over to the police. I also mentioned I'd made a copy of the journal, but suggested we just keep that between ourselves. I had a feeling my neighbor Elena Luna would not look too kindly on my even having read the journal— much less having my own personal copy.

Driving home it hit me how terribly wrong I'd been. Totally, terribly wrong. Michael Whitby had been up to his old tricks, as everyone knew he would be, while I struggled and worked to get him a place in the community. It wasn't that I felt betrayed by Whitby—I'd had no real faith in him and absolutely no relationship with him—it was more that I felt betrayed by my own values.

Did an individual have rights when that individual was bound and determined to cause pain again? But how could we stop it? Did we keep a man in prison his entire life because the recidivism rate for his crime was particularly high?

If the recidivism rate on pedophiles was 99 percent or 95 percent or 87 percent, depending on what literature you were reading, that meant that 1 percent or 5 percent or 13 percent of pedophiles *did* stop their crimes. Was it worth it? What percentage made it worthwhile? And who was to make that choice?

By the time I got back to the house, I was totally confused, totally depressed, and eager to think about my pending disease rather than the Michael Whitbys of this world.

Later that afternoon Megan came and crawled in my lap in the den where I sat with Willis watching TV. ''Mama,'' she said, her face serious, ''did you know Michael's daddy's dead?''

I nodded my head. ''Yes, honey, I knew that. Did Michael tell you?''

She nodded. "He said somebody killed him. Just like Bessie's other mommy and daddy, huh?"

"Yes, like that," I said. "But there's nothing to be afraid of," I said and kissed her cheek.

"But if Bessie's mommy and daddy could be killed like that, and Michael's daddy could be killed like that—"

"What, honey?" I asked, pulling her face away so I could look into her eyes.

"Are you gonna die, too?" she asked. "You and daddy?"

"We've talked about this, honey, how everybody and everything goes home to God. But with Daddy and me, it won't be until we're very, very old."

"Older'n Grandma?" she asked.

"Way older than Grandma. Because she's going to be around for a lot, lot longer."

"Then how come Bessie's mommy and daddy and Michael's daddy weren't real old when they died?"

"I guess God needed them in Heaven," I tried.

Megan sighed with the weight of the world. "What if God needs you and Daddy in Heaven? Huh? What then?"

"He doesn't, honey. Your daddy and I are going to be around for so long that you're going to have to feed us like we fed you when you were a baby."

"Yuck," she said. "Like baby food?"

"If my false teeth don't fit," I said, tickling her ribs.

She laughed. "You're gonna be like that lady in the cartoon with a phony leg and a wig and a glass eye and false teeth and—"

I tickled her until she couldn't talk she was laughing so hard. I kissed her forehead. "I love you," I said. "I'm gonna be around long enough to tell you you aren't raising your children right!"

"Yuck! I'm not going to have kids! Gross!" She jumped off my lap and headed for the stairs, screaming her sister's name at the top of her lungs.

I hadn't given her good answers; I'd just given her the only answers I had.

Nine

Arlene planned on taking Michael's journal to the police early Monday morning. I planned to beat Luna to McDonald's. I got the kids to bed, told Willis I had to go see his mother (I only lie because I have to, not because I want to), and hightailed it to McDonald's.

The store closed at nine on Sunday nights. I got there at eight-forty-five. There were more employees in the store than customers, and three of them could have been Michael Whitby's intended victim Mandy.

I went up to the counter and ordered an ice cream cone, asking the girl at the register which one was Mandy.

"I'm Mandy," she said.

She was a little thing, not much more than five feet tall, with a spare little body that hadn't filled out much. She had short blond hair, big teeth, and enormous, waiflike eyes.

"Mandy, if you can take a break, I'd love to buy you a soda—or anything else you want," I said.

She cocked her head at me. "Why? Do I know you?"

"It's about Michael Whitby," I said.

"Who?"

"Don't you know a man named Michael Whitby?"

"Oh!" She made a phony gagging noise. "Mike! That old creep, right?"

I described him. Mandy nodded her head. "Yeah, that's old beat-your-meat Mike, all right," she said. "That's what we call him here." Suddenly her face turned beet red. "Oh, gawd, he's not your old man or something, is he?" she asked.

I smiled. "Absolutely not." I pointed to a table by the window. "Do you have a minute to talk?"

She turned to one of the other girls. "Stace, I gotta talk to this lady for a minute. Cover for me, okay?"

The other girl nodded. Mandy grabbed an ice cream cone for herself and came out from behind the counter and followed me to a table.

We sat down with our cones, and I said, "I'm not sure if you've heard, but Michael Whitby was killed Saturday night."

Mandy's large eyes widened even further. "No shit?" she said. "Whoa. Car wreck? He drove like an idiot."

"No," I said. "He was murdered."

Mandy's eyes appeared to bug out in her head. "Really? Cool! How?"

"He was shot," I answered.

"Wow, did you see it?" she asked.

I ignored her question and instead asked her, "How well did you know him?"

"Man, I *didn't* know him! I mean, like he drove me home once and made a pass at me, but gross! He was old enough to be my father, ya know? And he kept calling me all the time! Really creepy. My mom's boyfriend told him to back off or he'd beat the shit out of him!" Her eyes got wide again. "Um, that's not how he died, is it?"

I shook my head. "No. Like I said, he was shot."

"Whew," she said. "I mean, Bert's a total asshole, but he's all my mom's got, ya know? Besides, he's paying the rent right now, so it would totally suck if he had to go to jail."

"Do you know who Michael Whitby was?" I asked.

"Well, ya know, the name's kinda familiar, but I only knew him by Mike." She giggled. "We called him beat-your-meat Mike 'cause he touched himself every time one of us girls walked by." She made the gagging noise again. "This guy was in total lack of a life, ya know?"

"I don't know if you read the local papers, Mandy, but Michael Whitby was a convicted child molester. There were a lot of editorials and stuff in the paper about him."

"No shit! A child molester? You mean he'd gone

to prison and everything?'' She grimaced. ''God, I knew the guy was creepy, but wait'll I tell the other girls. God, how gross!'' She looked at me, cocking her head again. ''So how did you get my name?''

''He mentioned it,'' I said.

Mandy sat back against the seat and dropped her cone on the table. ''He mentioned me? Like how?''

How much did I tell this child? Maybe it was time she knew that you don't play with grown men who touch themselves when young girls walk by.

''Your name was in his journal, Mandy. He seemed to think the two of you had a relationship. He mentioned driving you home one night.''

''Relationship my ass!'' the girl shouted. ''Like I said, he did—drive me home, I mean! But, shit, that's all! And he creeped me out totally! Trying to touch me all the goddamn time! Oh, this is sooooo gross!''

The girl Mandy had called Stace came over to the table. ''What's up, Mandy?'' she asked, handing her some napkins to clean up the spilled ice cream.

Mandy started telling Stace what I'd told her. Before she'd gotten too far, Stace was waving over the other employees. They all stood around the table, groaning, gagging, and otherwise enjoying themselves immensely at Michael Whitby's expense.

''And he wrote about me in his freakin' journal!'' Mandy told the others.

''Oh, God, like I am really creeped out!'' Stace said, while a girl named Melissa did an exaggerated shudder.

One of the boys said, "I told you that guy was a fruitcake!"

"And you three walking around wagging your asses at him! We told you!" another boy said.

"Wow, you think Bert did him?" the third boy asked.

Mandy sighed. "No, of course not! Bert's all talk and no walk. Hey, he pays the rent, that's about all you can ask for."

"Who do you think did it?" the third boy asked me.

"I don't know. I'm just glad that he never made any real contact with any of these girls," I said.

"Oh, like I'd let that freak touch me!" Stace said.

"No way!" Melissa said.

"If he tried anything for real with me," Mandy said, "I'd of broken off his schlong and fed it to him!"

"Great visual, Mandy!" one of the boys said.

I left the kids to their fun, going home happy that, this time at least, Michael Whitby had not succeeded.

None of these girls had been hurt by him; so now, instead of years of therapy and pain, they had a story to tell and that was all. He may have been close, but thank God close only counts in horseshoes and hand grenades.

The phone rang Monday while I was fixing myself some lunch. I picked it up and said, "Hello?"

"You have the right to remain silent, you have the right to an attorney—"

"Hey, Luna," I said, grinning, "what's up?"

"If you waive that right—"

"You saying I need to call Jim Bob Honeywell?" I asked, mentioning the name of my mother-in-law's gentleman caller—one of the five leading attorneys in the state of Texas.

"If I didn't have too damn much to do here as it is, Pugh, I'd be at your house in a New York minute and you'd be in cuffs so fast—"

"Luna, calm down," I said. "I'm really not following you."

"The hell you aren't! Guess who I just had an interview with?" she demanded.

"I really wouldn't know," I said.

"A girl by the name of Mandy Hogkins. Fifteen, small, blond, ring any bells?"

"Mandy Hogkins?" I said. "Hum . . ."

"Seems she was a little put out being dragged out of a class to be interviewed by the cops, since she already had an interview last night with a lady cop!"

"I never said I was a cop!" I said.

"I'm going to charge you this time, Pugh. Impersonating an officer! I swear to God I'm charging you!"

"I never, ever said I was a cop! I swear to you I didn't. I didn't tell her anything! I can't help what she assumed!"

"You know the old saying, 'assume makes an ass out of u and me'?" Luna said. "Well in this case it's gonna make a complete ass out of you! A jailbird ass! This time it won't be for any couple of hours! This time you're going down, baby! Down!"

I sighed. "Elena, I can't go to jail today. I have a doctor's appointment tomorrow—"

"I don't care if you have an audience with the pope tomorrow—" She stopped. "You finally going to have that pregnancy test?"

"I already did," I said. "It's . . . it's something else."

"What?"

"I can't talk about it—"

"Yeah, right," she said. "This surprises me! Haven't thought up a good excuse yet, huh, Pugh? Well, I'm not kidding around here—"

"Neither am I," I said. I sighed again. "It's called trophoblastic disease. Like a tumor. I have to have a D&C in the morning."

There was a silence on the other end of the line. Finally, she said, "I know you well enough to realize you wouldn't make up something like this to get out of a jam."

"No, I wouldn't," I said.

"Jesus," she said. "What can I do?"

"Keep your fingers crossed?" I suggested. "Vera's keeping the kids. Look, Luna, I'm sorry. But I really didn't say I was a cop. I'm not sure why Mandy would think I was one—"

"Forget it, Pugh, just forget it." There was another silence. "Have Willis call me tomorrow, okay?"

"Okay," I said, then heard a dial tone in my ear.

The rest of Monday flew by like a snail on downers in a heavy fog. I couldn't get my mind off what was planned for the next day. I tried to come up with suspects for Michael Whitby's murder, but most of me was saying, "Who cares? Tomorrow I find out if I have cancer!"

Arlene was still the best suspect—the wife always was. But what about Bert, Mandy's mother's boyfriend? Hell, I didn't get a last name for him, I thought. I hadn't even gotten a last name for Mandy. Luna had supplied that. Would Bert have known who "beat-your-meat" Mike really was? Did he find out and kill him when he discovered the real threat to his girlfriend's daughter?

What about the members of Rene Tillery's vigils? They were as big a bunch of suspects as anyone else. Hell, Rene would be the lead suspect! Except I really couldn't see Rene killing someone. Not unless a lynching party was involved. Then she'd have something to organize. Her husband Keith, on the other hand, I could see killing someone, but he didn't seem to really care enough about this issue to bother.

But what about Max and Carlie Galeana? Carlie had seemed at best half-hearted about the whole mess when she'd made her mission call to find out what Arlene Whitby and I had been up to at the grocery store; but what about Max? I had never talked to him, didn't know what his feelings were on the subject—if involvement had been his, Carlie's, or a joint decision.

Then there were the elusive Bowmans—those of the questionable genes. They seemed gung-ho about the vigils, but more as a community spirit kind of thing than as a "death to tyrants" kind of thing.

Rene's second in command, Tina Perlmutter, and

her husband Davis, I knew nothing about. At the one meeting where I'd met these people, Davis had seemed bored to tears, when he wasn't being a total jerk, while Tina, whom I'd met twice, seemed unable to do much without Rene's thumb up her butt.

That left nervous Abby Dane, whose daughter Rebecca was in Bessie's class. Did Abby's nervousness go beyond chewing her fingernails? At the best of times Abby saw bogeymen under the bed; would she hunt one down and shoot him if she were nervous enough? Especially after what Michael Whitby had said to her on my front porch the night he came to pick up Michael, Jr. What was it he had said? Something about Abby's daughter. Nothing more threatening, really, than just knowing she had one. Oh, and that she was blond. But there was no doubt in my mind that Abby took his comment as a threat. I probably would have too, under those circumstances.

But the real answer to all these questions and innuendoes was I didn't know. I just didn't know. These people were all just big blanks. I hadn't gotten involved enough in Rene's group—for obvious reasons—to get to know any of them.

But these people weren't the only ones in the community who had a problem with Michael Whitby. What about those teenagers who had been throwing rocks? Could they have escalated to gunfire? Passions run high with teenagers, especially when drinking's involved; what better night to be on the prowl with a couple of six packs and devilment in your heart than on Halloween? Take along a gun to shoot out streetlights and cause mischief; see the man who was terrorizing your mothers and sisters and girlfriends. It could happen. Easily. A group of boys, egging each other on. It had happened before.

Then, of course, there were the mothers and sisters and girlfriends themselves, not to mention fathers and brothers and boyfriends and husbands, and neighbors, and just plain pissed-off people in general.

It could have been anyone in the community. Black Cat Ridge or Codderville. Hell, it could have been someone who followed him from East Texas! Or, for that matter, any concerned person in the country who'd had more than they could take.

Michael Whitby was all over the news. His address was on the news. Anyone could have done this.

I suppose the surprise was just how long it had taken for someone to finally do it.

We took the kids into Codderville to a Mexican restaurant for dinner, then dropped them off at Vera's. This was a big treat—getting to spend a school night at Grandma's house. We'd told them the truth, more or less—Mommy had to go to the doctor early in the morning and Daddy had to drive her. My children, whose own lives were so exciting and full of adventure that they couldn't see beyond them, didn't ask for any details.

Willis and I got back to the house around nine. I packed a small bag; the procedure was supposed to be outpatient, but Marta Colman had said to bring a bag just in case. I packed a decent nightgown, robe, and found a pair of slippers that I'd worn in the hospital when Megan had been born. After I'd packed my toothbrush and minimum hair and face paraphernalia, I stole into the kitchen to my chocolate stash in the cabinet above the refrigerator, and packed a bag of Hershey's Kisses and a KitKat. Then I took out the KitKat and ate it standing at the kitchen sink.

It's hard to describe that night. The feelings I had—or the lack of them in some instances. I walked through the house like an android on cruise control. I picked at brown leaves on my plants, leaving the discarded waste wherever I happened to be, fluffed cushions on the sofas, picked up a toy on the floor and deposited it on the coffee table, as if this were an improvement.

I turned the TV on and off three times, and wandered upstairs looking for the kids—who, of course, were at Vera's.

Willis was having his own problems. We didn't talk much. I knew I was lucky. People had much worse prognoses than mine every day of the week. I mean, I had two very good chances—one, it could be benign, and secondly, even if it was malignant, it was easily treated.

But it didn't seem to mean much that night, waiting for the next day to come, pacing, and wandering, and wondering what my life would be like after tomorrow.

Finally Willis found me in the dining room, buffing the oak table with the sleeve of my nightgown.

Ten

Impressions: The interminable wait in the reception room, the papers filled out in triplicate. Voices on an intercom, muted laughter of a TV game show. My name being called; the sparseness of the small room with the bed, the cold of the hospital as I changed into a hospital gown, pushed my hair into a plastic cap, slipped the socklets on my feet. Marta Colman's smiling face, Willis's hand in mine. Ceiling tiles and a nurse with a needle.

Being wheeled down a long hall, counting light fixtures, talking silly. Marta Colman again, but just her eyes—the white mask covers her mouth and nose. A man she introduces as the surgeon. Just eyes. Cold eyes. I say something silly, the eyes warm up, crinkle with a smile under the mask. More drugs, they say, just a prick, you won't go under, just a local, can you feel this, good, that's good, somebody's golf score, the Rolling Stones in the background, good sounds, Doc, I say, or try to anyway.

I wake up back in the sparse room with the bed, Willis's hand in mine, Marta Colman's smiling face, no mask this time, everything was fine, just fine. I wake up again, Willis's hand in mine, you're okay, honey, thirsty, want a drink, oh yes, just a sip. Ice chips on my lips, Willis's hand in mine.

I sleep.

"The HCG levels haven't gone down as fast as I'd hoped," Marta Colman said.

We were in her office later that afternoon. Vera was picking the kids up from school. They were going to spend another night with her—basically so Willis and I could celebrate.

I was beginning to think maybe there wouldn't be anything to celebrate.

"Which means?" I asked.

Marta shrugged. "Too early to tell. I need you back in three weeks. We'll run another test. The levels should have started going down by then for sure. If they haven't gone down by then—and unless they've actually risen—we'll wait another three weeks and check again. After six weeks we'll have a better idea whether we need to go back in."

"And if they've risen?" I asked.

"Then we'll go back in. That would be a clear indicator of malignancy."

"And we won't know anything for at least another three weeks?" Willis asked.

"I'm sorry, y'all, I really am," Marta said, standing. "But that's the wonder of modern medicine. It's a great big ol' waiting game."

She smiled as she came around the desk, draping her arm over my shoulders. "But basically, don't worry. I know, I know, easy for me to say. But I'm serious. There's nothing to worry about at this stage." She opened the door and gave Willis a pointed look. "And no sex for three weeks, Mister. Got that?"

"Who, me?" Willis said, escorting me out. "Tell her. She's the aggressive one."

I smiled feebly and left the office.

Three more weeks of waiting. I told Willis on the way home that there was no need for Vera to keep the kids; I wanted them with me. Since there would be no celebrating that night—or any night in the very near future.

They weren't happy. I didn't care. We drove home with a sullen Graham and the girls constantly sniping at each other. It was music to my ears.

I left Willis with the kids and went to the grocery store, stocking up on as much food as I could get in the basket. I had great plans—big, fancy meals— cookbook dishes and real pyramid meals with every one of the food groups represented. They were going to miss me when I was gone, by God.

Willis put up the groceries while I gathered every article of dirty clothing in the house—even things the kids had outgrown—and did marathon laundry. I scrubbed the floors in the kitchen and cleaned out under the sink in the downstairs bath. If Willis was going to entertain at my funeral, I'd be damned if anyone would get the chance to say something nasty about my housekeeping.

Willis stopped me when I took the toothbrush to the grout in the entry hall tiles.

"What are you doing?" he asked, pulling me up off my knees.

"Cleaning!" I said, resisting his arms and trying to get back to my knees. He finally got me to an upright position, which had me looking into the dining room. "Oh, my God. Look at those windows!" I said, heading toward them.

"Stop!" he shouted. "What the hell are you doing?"

"Cleaning!" I said again. "What does it look like?"

"What does it look like? I'll tell you what it looks like! It looks like you are obsessing!"

I rolled my eyes. "I just think the house should be clean," I said.

"Why?" my husband asked. "It's never been clean before."

"You've always thought I was a lousy house-keeper, haven't you?" I said, tears stinging my eyes.

"Yes," he said, taking me in his arms. "You *are* a lousy housekeeper. So am I. This is not a bad thing."

He pulled me toward the living room and we sat down together on the couch. "If you die," he said, reading my mind, "I'll use your life insurance to hire someone to clean before the open house."

I leaned my head against his shoulder. "Good idea," I said, and burst into tears.

"Eej, you're not dying," he said, kissing my hair.

"I know," I said between sobs.

"Then why are you doing this?" he asked.

I looked into his eyes. "Raging hormones?" I asked.

"Wouldn't be the first time," he said.

I'd let him have that one—for a little while.

I had three weeks to obsess—or I could do something creative. Like find out who killed Michael Whitby. This was not the first time I'd stuck my nose in police business—but it would be the first time I'd done it when there was no real need. Other than to keep my mind off something else. Always before a friend or a family member needed me. I could justify myself, I suppose, by saying Arlene Whitby needed me. That Michael, Jr., needed me. But even I knew that wouldn't be the truth. I was doing this purely and only to keep my mind occupied.

Better than taking up tennis.

I decided to start with the members of Rene Tillery's group. Bessie's class was going on a field trip to a nearby organic farm that Thursday, which gave me a perfect excuse to talk with Abby Dane, the nervous single mother whose daughter was in the same class. I volunteered as a replacement chaperone as soon as I found out Abby was already on the list.

Thursday dawned cool and crisp, with bright sunshine promising a warmer afternoon. I dressed the kids in layers and then drove all three to school, parking the car in the lot and going with Bessie to her class.

One nice thing about having children the age of my girls is they're still proud to have parents. They're not yet embarrassed by your existence—which happens when they get to be my son Graham's age. I believe he tells people he was hatched, not born.

Bessie held my hand proudly as we entered her room. She introduced me to some of the girls standing around, who were awestruck at the fact that I was Bessie's mother. Mrs. Jorgenson, Bessie's teacher, waved abstractedly at me as she tried to get her class calmed down.

I shooed Bessie to her seat and went to join Abby Dane and another mother who were standing against the wall behind Mrs. Jorgenson's desk, awaiting instructions.

Abby smiled and gave me a finger wave as I took up space next to them. The other mother I didn't know, and we hastily whispered introductions while Mrs. Jorgenson warned her charges about the rules and regs of today's field trip.

Micky Cross, the other mother, was dressed like me—jeans, running shoes, T-shirt, and down jacket. The nineties mom look. Abby, however, was dressed in preppie splendor. Her short blond hair was pulled back with a black velvet headband, her khakis were crisp and her sweater vest argyle. Under the sweater vest she wore a buttoned down Oxford cloth shirt, and her feet were covered in matching argyle socks and oxblood Bass loafers. Somehow, none of this

went with the pointy, foxlike face and the chewed-
to-the-quick fingernails.

Half an hour later, clipboard in hand, I was mark-
ing off nametags as fourth-graders boarded the bus
for New Age Farms. Abby was inside the bus, making sure the children actually sat down two to a seat,
while Micky Cross helped the bus driver pack up
lunches and sundry items. Mrs. Jorgenson—and
please don't quote me on this—was on the other
side of the bus sneaking a cigarette.

We got the kids on and took our seats in the front
of the bus. I grabbed the seat next to Abby, leaving
Micky Cross to sit next to Mrs. Jorgenson.

After we had gotten underway, I leaned toward
Abby and said, "Well, I guess Rene's got something
to say about the way things turned out."

Abby looked at me nervously. "She said we
weren't supposed to talk to you," she said.

I nodded. "I'm sure that was before—well, you
know."

Abby sighed and leaned toward me. "God, wasn't
that awful! I don't think any of us meant for that to
happen!" she said, then giggled. "Well, maybe none
of us except Rene!"

"How's she taking it?" I asked.

Abby shook her head. "Like she's won, how
else?"

"Well, I guess she has, in a way."

"I'm just so glad it's all over," Abby said. "I
mean, I wouldn't wish that on a dog, but at least
we don't have to worry about him anymore."

"Certainly seems convenient," I said.

Abby giggled. "I have to agree—the timing couldn't have been better!"

"Has to make you wonder, though. I mean, who would do such a thing?"

"Whoever it was deserves a medal as far as I'm concerned!" Abby said, her voice vehement. "I mean, I know that wasn't the right answer, but, by God, it was an answer!"

"Surely you don't condone—"

"Of course not," she whispered fiercely, "but it's over now! That's the main thing!"

"Who do you think did it?" I asked.

Abby pulled away and gave me a look. "I'm sure I wouldn't know," she said. Then she turned and looked out the window, dismissing me and my not-so-hidden agenda.

New Age Farms was a small-sized spread by Texas standards—only about five hundred acres. They supplied the local grocery stores with organic carrots, kale, and an assortment of organic herbs, and had a two-hundred-acre organic apple orchard. The buildings were all of rock, even the barns and outbuildings—some seemingly as old as the land itself; others obviously new but designed in such a way as to blend in with the old.

I could only assume the owners of the farm made as much money from the tours—such as the one we were taking today—as they did from their organic farms. They had a petting "farm"—no zoos in the new age—with piglets, small goats, calves, chickens, ducks, and a miniature horse about the size of a Great Dane, and their lectures on nutrition and the righteousness of organic foods were done with the use of song and puppets. The hay wagon for the mandatory hay ride was pulled by two big, beautiful Clydesdales.

The kids loved it. Hell, I loved it. Before lunch, the kids were led to the milking shed where they got to watch the cows being milked, and all the kids, except for the lactose-intolerant ones, of course, got to drink that very milk with the lunches they brought with them from home. Dessert was ice cream made from the milk of the same cows.

There was only room on the hay wagon for two adults, and I opted to stay behind as soon as I learned Abby had no intention of getting on the wagon. "Allergies," she said.

We sat down at a picnic table in the sun and waited.

"I'm sorry if I offended you earlier," I began. "This whole thing just has me very curious."

Abby waved my apologies aside. "No offense taken." She sighed. "It's just Rene. She really has a thing about you, E.J."

I grinned—sheepishly, I hope. "We had words," I said.

"So I gathered. And I've got to tell you, she was as upset as I was about Michael Whitby being at your house that day I was there."

I sighed. "I wanted to explain that to you. Michael, Jr., is in my other daughter's class. He came over to play and instead of his mother picking him up like she was supposed to, Michael Sr. showed up," I said.

Abby shook her head. "Well, I'm sure that was awful for you and all, but I can't help but think you brought it on yourself, E.J.'' She shuddered. "God, that man! The things he said to me!''

I nodded my head. "It was pretty bad. But Abby, I have to tell you, I hated the way that boy and his mother were being treated.''

Abby nodded. "The boy, yes.'' She shook her head. "But that mother! I mean, really, E.J.! I divorced my husband and I'm doing fine! You don't see me staying with a no-good! And all my ex ever did was sleep with his secretary!''

"We all react differently, Abby. That's why we're called individuals,'' I said. Okay, a little self-righteously.

Still, Abby shook her head. "No! You don't stay with a man who abuses children! You just don't!''

I had to agree with her. I didn't understand it either. But I wasn't raised in a restrictive religion with parents who taught me the absolutes that Arlene Whitby's parents had taught her. There was something to be said for walking a mile in another's shoes.

"The wife probably killed him,'' Abby said. "Hell, I would have!''

"I don't think so,'' I said. "I've been thinking about it a lot and—''

Abby gave me a look. "I hear you do this—get involved in stuff like this. Murder, I mean. Doesn't it scare you?''

"I guess my curiosity is stronger than the fear,'' I said.

Abby gave a shudder. "Well, you won't ever see me hanging around where a murder's occurred! It gives me the creeps!''

I grinned. "Yeah, but doesn't it make you wonder? I mean, here we all were, this whole group of us with one goal—to get rid of Michael Whitby, and then, voila, he's gone."

"But we didn't have anything to do with it!" Abby protested.

"What makes you think that?" I asked.

Abby just stared at me. Finally, she whispered, "Are you suggesting one of our group was responsible for that man's murder?" She looked around to make sure no one had heard. As far as I could tell, only one of the goats from the kiddie farm was even within earshot.

"You said yourself, Abby, that the timing was very good."

"Yes, but—"

"*Someone* killed him," I said. "Why not one of our group?"

"But who?" she whispered, again looking around.

I shrugged. "I really don't know any of the participants that well, Abby. But you do. What do you think?"

Abby stood up and walked away from me, her back to me. Finally, she turned and looked at me. "Are you trying to get me to rat out my friends?" she asked. "Is that the right vernacular?"

"Sounds accurate," I said. I stood up too, walking towards her. "I didn't realize these people were your friends, Abby. I thought you just joined the group as a concerned parent."

"I did! But I knew Tina from before. She's a neighbor. She and Davis live two doors down from me. And I knew Rene slightly of course. Who doesn't know Rene if they have a child in Black Cat Elementary?'' She put her hands on her hips and glared at me. ''And what makes you think it's got to be someone in our group? Hell, the entire community wanted that guy out of the way! It could have been anybody! And if you want my opinion, I still think it was the wife! It usually is, you know. That's what they say on TV. The spouse is usually the one!''

''I don't think so in this case,'' I said.

''Well, what do you know?'' Abby said. ''You might stick your nose in this kinda stuff all the time, E.J., but that doesn't make you an expert!''

''I'm not saying I'm an expert, Abby. I just don't feel that Arlene did it. I can't really tell you why; just that I don't think she has it in her.''

Abby sighed. ''I can't believe you want me to rat out my friends.''

I shook my head. ''I'm not asking you to do that.''

She laughed. ''You're not?''

I shrugged and laughed back. ''Okay, I guess I am,'' I admitted.

Abby took a long breath, letting it out slowly. ''Well, I could tell you a few things about Davis Perlmutter—'' she started, but then we both turned as we heard the heavy clomp of the Clydesdales and the giggles and yells of the fourth-graders as the hay wagon returned.

The few things about Davis Perlmutter were going to have to wait.

Eleven

I was late getting on the bus on our way back and ended up sitting next to Mrs. Jorgenson, who spent the entire forty-five-minute ride to Black Cat Ridge telling me what a wonder I had in Bessie. All I could do was agree. Bessie's position as teacher's pet—year after year after year after year—had her siblings in a bit of a snit, but I must admit she's the only one of my children I never dread having a parent teacher conference about. Bessie will either grow up to replace Mother Teresa or be one of the few female serial killers. At this point it's hard to tell which.

Needless to say, I never had a chance to quiz Abby Dane regarding her remarks about Davis Perlmutter. I couldn't help but wonder what those "few things about Davis Perlmutter" were. Was he in the habit of going around shooting neighborhood bores and bullies? *That* would solve a lot a problems.

Or maybe he had his own problems along the lines of Michael Whitby's. It seemed to be more common than most parents would want to believe. Or he could be a wife beater. Tina was rather quiet and self-effacing. She let Rene lead her around by the nose. She could definitely have a little "battered woman syndrome" going there. But what would that have to do with Michael Whitby?

I waited in Bessie's classroom with her until the bell sounded, then rounded up the kids and headed for the high school to pick up Luna's boys.

By the time we got home, I was itching to know all about Davis Perlmutter. Maybe he'd been Michael Whitby's cellmate in Huntsville. I mean, how many ex-cons did we have living in Black Cat Ridge? A month ago I would have said none, but who ever really knows these things?

Or maybe—and oh, I liked this!—Davis Perlmutter was going under the name "Bert" and had a second home in Codderville, living with Mandy Hogkins and her mother. That would make *so* much sense! This was a scenario I could really get my teeth into.

I called Abby Dane as soon as the kids were busy elsewhere. She picked up on the second ring.

"Hello?"

"Abby, hi, it's E.J."

There was a silence.

"E.J. Pugh," I said.

"Yes," she said, her voice cold.

"I was hoping we could finish our conversation," I said.

"We did," Abby said, and hung up in my ear.

I had a sneaking suspicion Abby had talked to Rene Tillery at some point between that earlier conversation and now.

Rene really had it in for me, and I had to wonder why. Sure, we disagreed on the main issue at hand; but was that reason enough to sabotage me at every turn? Well, for Rene, yes, it probably was. On the other hand, if she had something to hide, there would be even more reason to sabotage me.

I liked this scenario almost as much as the Davis/Bert scenario. Rene Tillery, in a fit of community fervor, took a gun and blew a hole in Michael Whitby's head.

On Halloween.

When she should have been out with her daughters trick or treating.

Okay, maybe it wasn't a great scenario. I wondered how much my heart was really in this.

I got a pad and wrote down a schedule: I could tackle Max and Carlie Galeana at church on Sunday. That left the Tillerys, the Perlmutters, and the Bowmans. I doubted seriously if Rene would speak to me—and probably Tina Perlmutter would follow Rene's lead. But the Bowmans—at the least, maybe I'd find out which was which. I picked up the phone and dialed.

"The Bowmans are coming over for drinks tonight," I informed my husband when he walked in the door that evening.

"Do what?" he said.

"You know. Pat and Lee. Drinks. This evening."

"Why would we have drinks with the Bowmans?" he asked. "We don't even know which one is which!"

"This would be a perfect way to find out," I said, smiling as I set the table for dinner.

"Uh-uh," Willis said. "You're up to something."

"Who me?" I asked innocently. "I just thought we haven't been entertaining nearly enough."

"Okay, fine," he said. "If you want to entertain, invite a couple we actually like!"

"What's wrong with Pat and Lee?" I asked, going to the stove to put the contents of a pot in a serving dish.

"They're boring," Willis said. "They're not particularly bright, and we have absolutely nothing in common."

"Now how would you know that?" I asked, taking the serving dish to the table.

"Because I spent several incredibly boring nights with them on the picket line! They were both terribly excited one night about a new dry cleaner moving into town!"

"Well, we only have one dry cleaner now, honey. Competition is always nice."

Willis sat down at the table and glared at me. "Okay, what are you *really* up to?" he asked.

I went to the foot of the stairs and called up to the children, letting them know dinner was ready. When I turned, Willis was right behind me. I put my hands on his chest to keep from running into him.

"You're up to something," he said.

I moved around him back to the kitchen.

"I don't know what it is," he said, "but I obviously would not approve or you'd tell me."

I took the chicken out of the oven and put it on a hot pad on the table.

"Smells good, huh?" I said. "Your mother gave me the recipe."

"What time are we expecting our company?" he asked.

"In about an hour and a half," I said.

"Are you going to tell me ahead of time why we're doing this, or am I just supposed to wing it?"

All three kids came barreling in the kitchen at that moment, trying to beat each other to the table and screaming at the tops of their lungs while they were about it. It was an efficient way to duck Willis's question.

They were both wearing blue jeans, sweatshirts, and matching Birkenstock sandals—no floral shoelaces this time to tell which was the female. It wasn't until I got a profile look as I escorted the couple into the living room that I surmised the one in the red sweatshirt was the Mrs. There was a definite outline of boobs. Now if I just knew which was Pat and which was Lee, the evening might go a little smoother.

The kids were upstairs doing their homework—or pretending to, depending on the kid—and I brought out a decent bottle of wine and a cheese plate. The Mrs. was going on at some length about Thanksgiving decorations for the middle school—a project for which she appeared to be in charge—and her husband was giving her his undivided attention.

When she took a breath, her husband beamed at her. "Pat's really good at that stuff," he said.

Willis and I exchanged a look and both broke into grins. "Well, Lee," Willis said, addressing the male, "what do you think of the Cowboys' chances at the championship?"

We did that for a while, went on to the weather, did five minutes on favorite restaurants in the greater Codderville area, segued into "recipes I have known and loved," meandered through "something funny my child did recently," until I was finally able to bring up the reason for the invitation in the first place.

Pat was on her second glass of wine, Lee on his third, when I said, "So what do you think of this whole Michael Whitby fiasco?"

Lee barked a laugh. "Well, nothing much more for poor Rene to organize, is there?" he said.

"Oh, Lee," Pat said, slapping her husband on the leg and giggling. "Be nice."

"Weird, huh?" Willis said. After I'd clued him in after dinner, he'd reluctantly agreed to take a role in the proceedings. "I can't believe somebody just shot him."

"Why not?" Lee said. "Anybody deserved shooting, that man did."

"Who do you think did it?" Pat asked, leaning forward and beating me to the question of the minute.

I shook my head. "I've been thinking about that,"

I said, "but I haven't come up with anything." I leaned forward too. "What about you?"

Pat giggled. "Well, I'd say Rene, but when you think about it, what happened just ruined all her fun."

Lee barked another laugh. "And you're telling me to be nice?"

"Oh, hush," Pat said, slapping her husband's leg again. (I had this image of a giant, permanent bruise on the poor man's thigh.) "I just can't imagine who'd actually do it," she said. "Other than a man."

"Why a man?" Willis asked.

"A woman would have been more subtle than a gunshot through the head," Pat said. "Poison, maybe. Or a nice little automobile accident. Now, that's the way I'd have done it. Sever the brake line in his car. Simple, easy, and if the car blew up it would be hard to discover."

Lee gave his wife a look. "Glad to know you've been giving this so much thought," he said.

"That'll teach you to be a good boy," Pat said, then slapped him on the leg again.

I winced.

"What about you, Lee?" Willis asked. "Who do you think did it?"

"Abby Dane," he said without missing a beat.

"Abby?" I asked, almost laughing out loud. "Why?"

"The least likely suspect," he said. "You ever read Agatha Christie? I'm a big fan. It's always the person you least suspect. Gotta be Abby Dane. Who would think a Milquetoast woman like that would have the nerve to blow somebody's brains out, huh?'' He laughed and slapped his own knee.

''Well, if this was fiction, maybe,'' I said. ''But who do you *really* think did it?''

Lee and Pat looked at each other, then both looked back at me. ''The wife,'' they said in unison.

''Always the spouse,'' Lee said.

''Amen to that,'' Pat said. ''This pokey-joe—'' she said, pointing her thumb towards Lee ''—ever goes under suspicious circumstances, you best look my way.''

The two laughed and slapped each other on the shoulders.

The conversation moved on to movies—they preferred the *Beavis and Butthead* variety—books—true crime for her, anything to do with computers for him (fiction or nonfiction)—when was the best time to plant bulbs, and finally little league soccer. By that time, it was ten o'clock and I was making noises about getting the kids to bed.

The Bowmans took the hint and headed for the door, inviting Willis and me over to their house that weekend—''Sorry, we're going out of town''—to go to the movies together the following week—''We'll have to get back to you''—and maybe some Chinese sometime soon.

We got them out the door, and I leaned against it after it had closed, sighing.

''It was your idea,'' Willis said.

''You think we can prove they did it?'' I asked. ''Just as a community service?''

''Be nice,'' he said, and slapped me on the shoulder.

*   *   *

Sunday morning didn't exactly dawn, it just sort of drizzled in. Sleet was hitting the windows, the sky was dreary and overcast, and the temperature was in the low forties. Unusual, but not unheard of weather for this early in November in this part of Texas. Basically, in Texas you can have any kind of weather you want, just none of it for very long—except of course heat. Heat we have twenty-four/seven, for months and months and months on end.

The kids took one look out the windows and refused to go to church. Since Willis was firmly on their side, which he proved by snuggling deeper under the covers and giving me a petulant ''no'' every time I suggested he get up, I decided to forego my intended interview with Max and Carlie Galeana. I consoled myself with the thought that it might be better to tackle Carlie on her own. Max was really an unknown entity; Carlie, on the other hand, had that guilt thing going about having called me with the lie for Rene Tillery.

If there's one thing I learned at my mother's knee it was how to take someone else's guilt feelings and run with them.

We spent the rest of that Sunday in separate activities—Willis and Graham watching the Cowboys game, the girls attempting to teach Puddin'—our half-Rottweiler, half–basset hound—to roll over and play dead, and me in the master bedroom with a good book and a stash of chocolate.

Monday was almost as miserable weatherwise as Sunday. It was no longer sleeting, but the temperature was down to the midthirties and the sky was still the same gunmetal gray it had been the day before. The highlight was that the children had to go to school and Willis had to go to work.

I called Carlie Galeana on my cell phone on my way back from taking the kids to school and asked her over to my house for a coffee klatch around ten. She accepted and I hightailed it to the grocery store to pick up something homemade-looking in their bakery.

They had some nice cinnamon rolls, which I took home, put on a fancy plate, stuck in the microwave for a minute to warm, then put on the table. I sprayed the kitchen with some cinnamon air freshener to give it that ''just cooked'' smell, then stuck some coffee on to brew.

Carlie showed up ten minutes early. When I opened the door, she said, ''God, I was hoping you'd call! We've got to figure out who did this!''

She brushed past me and headed for the kitchen. This wasn't going to be so bad, I told myself.

She sat down at the table and grabbed one of the buns. ''Food Giant?'' she asked.

I nodded.

She grinned. ''Tried to fool me with the fancy plate, huh?''

''You're too quick for me, Carlie,'' I said. ''Coffee or tea?''

''Coffee. Black. Two Equals if you have it.'' She picked up a cinnamon roll and stared at it. ''I shouldn't eat this, you know. It's not on my diet.''

''What diet are you on now?'' I asked, bringing two mugs and the box of Equal to the table.

''Pritikin. Again. Or still. I'm not sure. I did Atkins for a while, but all that protein messed up my regularity. Have you heard about the cabbage soup diet?''

"I've heard—"

She held up a hand. "Don't. Sucks. Trust me." She took a bite of cinnamon roll. "Now," she said, after washing down half a roll with a sip of coffee. "Back to the important stuff. Who do you think did it?"

I rolled my eyes. "That's why I asked you here, Carlie. To find out who *you* think did it!"

Carlie shrugged. "The wife's the first one to pop to mind."

I sighed. "Everybody says that. Not only is it too easy, I just don't see it. Arlene's not the type."

Carlie shook her head. "She could have you snookered, E.J. You don't really know this woman. Your bleeding heart just has you feeling sorry for her."

"Well, Carlie, let's don't beat around the bush here," I said.

"Hey, the last time I talked to you I told a great big ol' fib. I told myself I wouldn't do that with you again. You strike me as the so-honest-it-hurts type, E.J. So that's what I'm doing. I'm being honest."

"Fine," I said. We shook on it. "I'll be honest, too. I really don't think Arlene did it. For one thing, she had nothing to gain. She already had all the heat from his reputation, and as far as I can tell, there wasn't any money in it for her. Besides which, she's seriously religious and she thought of Whitby as her cross to bear."

"Um. The martyr type? Enjoying her pain?"

"Maybe," I said, shrugging, "or maybe just too emotionally whipped by life to be able to do anything about it."

"Okay, fine," Carlie said, pushing back the plate of cinnamon rolls. "Let's put Arlene on the back burner for now. Who does that leave? Besides every right-thinking person in a fifty-mile radius?"

"Right now I'm concentrating on Rene Tillery's vigilante group," I said.

Carlie rolled her eyes. "We weren't vigilantes," she said. "Just concerned parents! God, E.J., don't start!"

"Okay, bad choice of words. Rene's group. How's that?"

"Okay, I agree that's a starting place. Are we agreed that shooting Whitby between the eyes isn't Rene's style?"

"Agreed," I said. "Pat Bowman suggested it had to be a man. She said a woman would be more subtle."

"Oh, Pat's the wife? I thought it was the other way around!"

"No, this is definite. She's Pat; he's Lee."

"Oh, shit," Carlie said. "I talked to her on the phone the other day and I called her Lee."

"Are you sure it was her? Their voices are almost identical," I said.

"Hum, good point. Whoever it was answered to the name, so maybe I was talking to him. Anyway, I like her thought. I do want to believe we as a sex would be more creative than a simple gunshot to the head."

"So, that narrows the field down to the men. I can say unequivocably it wasn't Willis—" I started.

"Why?" Carlie asked.

I laughed. "Because he's my husband and I know him. He didn't do it."

"That's all well and good, E.J., but we can't just eliminate someone because he's someone else's husband. That lets all the guys out."

"You think *your* husband did it?" I asked her.

"I sure don't want to think so, but, hey, who knows?" she said shrugging. "There are a lot of things we don't know about these guys."

I thought about what she said for a moment— then quickly dismissed it. I knew everything there was to know about Willis Pugh. I knew what he was capable of and what he wasn't. I knew he'd shoot someone in a heartbeat if they were accosting the children or me; I also knew that if he ran over a kitten on a dark and lonely road, he'd spend an hour looking for the owner.

Carlie Galeana may have her doubts about her husband, but I had none about mine.

"So why do you think Max did it?" I asked her.

She choked on the coffee she'd just taken into her mouth. "I didn't say Max did it!" she screeched.

"Well, I know Willis didn't."

"All I said E.J. is that if we asked Lee—"

"Pat—"

"Pat, she'd say Lee didn't do it, and if we asked Tina, she'd say Davis didn't do it, and if we asked Rene, she'd say Keith didn't do it. So who do we believe?"

"You've got a point," I allowed. "But Willis still didn't do it."

"Okay, fine," she said, sighing, "if Willis isn't a suspect, then neither is Max."

"Fine. That leaves Lee, Keith, and Davis."

"And Abby."

"Abby?" I said. "Don't tell me because she's the least likely suspect?"

Carlie gave me a puzzled look. "No," she said. "Because she threatened to kill Whitby the day before Halloween."

Twelve

I choked on my own mouthful of coffee. "Threatened to kill him?" I said. "What? When? Where?"

"Why and who? Oh, and how. Seriously, we were at Rene's for a meeting on Friday, the day before Halloween, and the subject was, of course, Michael Whitby, and Abby said, and I quote, 'Why don't we just kill the asshole?'"

I rolled my eyes. "Who in that group hasn't said that out loud more than once?" I asked.

"Granted," she said, "but it was the *way* Abby said it, I guess, that made me remember it."

"Like how?" I asked.

Carlie shrugged. "It's hard to describe. It was like—Well, she meant it. It came across as a serious question. 'Why don't we just kill him?'"

"Well, if it was a serious question then she obviously thought the group should do it—as a project, I suppose. Do you think she'd make that proposal to the group and then the very next day just go do it herself?''

Carlie shrugged again. "I don't know. You're probably right." She sighed. "But somebody had to do it!''

"Agreed. We keep eliminating people just because neither of us can imagine someone we know doing this," I said.

"Like our own husbands," she said, giving me a look.

"Don't start," I said.

"But you know," Carlie said, "what Pat said is just so much hogwash! Terribly sexist when you think about it. Women use guns more and more these days. Hell, even I've been to the range! I can't say it's exactly my forte—I couldn't hit the broad side of a barn—but I know plenty of women who can.''

"True. You think Pat was covering for herself?"

"Ah-ha!" Carlie said, a grin spreading across her face. "We could be on to something! She gets us focusing on the men while she calmly cleans her gun of fingerprints!''

"Well, if she has a gun, it *should* have her fingerprints on it," I said.

"Oh, you know what I mean! Cleaning it, period. So it'll look like it hasn't been fired.''

I sighed. "Pat Bowman walking up to Michael Whitby, putting a gun to his head, and pulling the trigger." I shook my head. "I just can't see it.''

"I can't see anybody doing it, E.J., but somebody did!"

"What we need, Carlie, are facts, not suppositions."

Carlie frowned. "Well, that's fine for you to say. But where are we supposed to get them?"

"We need alibis."

"Christ, it was Halloween! Everybody was out with their kids."

"Or home, supposedly holding down the fort."

"Well, yes, Max took the kids out and I stayed with the candy dish."

I grinned. "So what's your alibi, Carlie?"

She tore off a corner of cinnamon bun and threw it at me. "Four hundred and eleven devils, angels, princesses, and Power Rangers. All at my door in a steady stream from seven until after ten."

"So you say," I said.

Carlie stood up. "Well, this is getting us nowhere fast."

"You're on good terms with Rene, right?"

Carlie looked to the heavens for support. "Don't ask me!"

I stood up too. "Why don't you call her? See if you can find out what she knows, and where she was Halloween. After the thing at the school. I saw her there briefly, but that was early."

"You asked me, didn't you? You really asked me!"

"You know I can't do it. She won't speak to me. Oh, and Tina Perlmutter, too."

"Would you like me to come over and cook dinner for you tonight? Maybe read your children a bedtime story?''

''Your sarcasm is wasted on me,'' I said, leading her toward the door.

''Rene's right, E.J. You *are* an evil woman,'' she said, heading toward her car.

''Don't forget it,'' I called after her. ''I have ways of making people regret not doing as I tell them,'' I said, then tried for an evil cackle. I don't think it worked too well.

Carlie rolled her eyes and headed home.

There was one possibility greater, I thought, than the members of Rene Tillery's group. And that was the Berts of this world. Maybe not Bert himself— the boyfriend of Mandy Hogkins's mother—but the fathers of the girls Michael Whitby abused or had on his list to be abused.

I had to wonder what Whitby's modus operandi was. Did he concentrate on stalking one girl at a time, or did he have a backup? Mandy was the only girl mentioned in Whitby's journal, but could there have been another? Maybe even another journal? Maybe he kept a journal per girl.

But in reading his journal, I got the impression this was the first time he'd kept one—and that he was doing it by order of his court-appointed psychologist.

What had he done before—back in East Texas? I had to wonder if those girls had been one at a time or overlapping? I knew someone who might be able to tell me, but I also knew Elena Luna didn't like to part with information—especially to me.

Being a glutton for punishment, I called her anyway.

"Luna," she said, picking up on the first ring.

"Hi, it's E.J."

"How did the surgery go?" she asked immediately.

I'd forgotten to call her. Like I'd tried to forget about the surgery. "Everything went well," I said. "The HCG levels—the hormones—haven't gone down yet, so I have another three weeks to wait."

"It's probably okay," she said.

"Probably," I agreed.

"Are you okay?"

"You mean mentally? As well as can be expected. I'm trying to keep myself occupied, which is the other reason I called," I said, hoping to sound as if the real reason was to ease her mind on my physical condition.

"Why do I know I'm going to regret being nice to you?" she said.

"Don't be like that. You agree I should keep my mind occupied, don't you?"

"Yes, I do. That's why I suggest you take up quilting. It's all the rage now, I hear. Keep your mind and your fingers busy."

"I don't sew."

"Books. You were an English major. Read. Or better yet, you're supposed to be a writer—write."

"What's this 'supposed to' business?"

"How much have you written lately, huh? Don't you have a deadline or something to keep you busy?"

"Come on, Luna. I just have one simple question," I said.

"Your questions are never simple and you never have just one."

"What was Whitby's MO with the girls in East Texas? I mean, was it one girl, then on to another, or did he overlap?"

"I cannot discuss an open case with you, Pugh."

"It's not an open case. Whitby served his time for his crimes in East Texas, right? Those cases are closed. I'm asking about old business here, Luna."

"You're asking about none of your business, Pugh. Like always."

I sighed. "What would it hurt, Elena? It's a simple question."

"Not so simple. I don't know the answer. I'd have to look it up."

"Okay," I said. "I'll wait."

"No, you won't because I'm hanging up. I haven't got time to run errands for you. Goodbye, Pugh. And just hold on. You're going to be fine."

She hung up in my ear.

Which was more or less what I'd expected. But somehow I thought that information could be important. If there was someone besides Mandy who Whitby had been stalking, I needed to find out who she was—and who her loved ones were.

Concentrating on Rene's vigilante group was getting me nowhere fast. I did agree with Carlie that Pat's theory on only men using a gun—that a woman would be more subtle—was hogwash. Women could be just as stupid and unsubtle as a man. Maybe not as often, but I knew it could happen. But Carlie's theory that Pat was trying to lead me away from herself was nothing more than a theory—more than likely, Pat's scenario was just her opinion.

But the fact that someone could be lying to me was not lost on me. Of course someone could be lying. Hell, Carlie said she couldn't shoot the broad side of a barn—and whose word did I have on that? Carlie's. That was the problem with asking questions. Even when you did get answers, you couldn't always believe them. Not to mention Carlie's own suspicion of her husband. Well, maybe not suspicion, but she certainly didn't seem to be as sure of his innocence as I was of Willis's.

Maybe I should have a little chat with Max Galeana—not to mention Davis Perlmutter.

I checked my watch. It was almost time for the kids to get out of school. There was another lead I needed to follow up before I got to Max and Davis. I wondered if the kids would like to go by McDonald's for an afternoon snack.

I was in luck. The store wasn't terribly crowded and Mandy was there, lazily dipping french fries in hot grease.

I got all the kids ice cream cones, sat them down at two tables—Graham and Luna's boys at one and my girls at the other—and headed toward the counter to talk to Mandy.

As I did, a man stood up with his tray, blocking my path as he headed for the trash cans.

"Keith?" I said.

He turned and looked at me, then smiled. "Hey,

E.J. Boy, are you in trouble with my wife," he said, his grin wide.

"Please tell her I'm not the devil incarnate," I said.

He shook his head. "I could tell her that, E.J., but she's not going to believe me. Although she should calm down now, what with that asshole dead and everything getting back to normal."

"How can things get back to normal when someone's been murdered, Keith?" I asked.

He laughed and patted me on the back. "Honey, your pinko bleeding heart's showing again."

He headed for the trash can and out the door, with me fuming behind him. I hate being patronized, and I think I just got a big dose of it.

I went up to the counter and called Mandy's name.

Seeing me, she rolled her eyes. "You again?" she said, obviously not thrilled to see me.

"Hey, Mandy, how you doing?" I said, a big smile on my face.

"I've answered as many questions about that old fart as I'm going to," she stated, hands on hips and a frown on her face. "And you're not even a cop!" she said, accusingly.

"I never said I was," I said. "Actually, I'm just a concerned citizen."

"Well concern this!" she said, making a decidedly unladylike gesture.

"How about I pay you ten bucks for the information?" I asked.

She looked at me, blinked, and said, "Okay."

She came out from behind the counter and joined

me at my own separate table. The kids were paying no attention, as usual, to whatever their mother and or next-door neighbor was up to.

"Now what?" she asked, holding her hand out for the money.

I put a five on her outstretched palm. "The other five when we finish," I said.

She rolled her eyes. "I think I saw this in a movie once," she said.

"Probably," I agreed. "Okay, now here's my question: Tell me about Bert."

"That's not a question," she said.

I reached out for the five and she promptly stuffed it in the pocket of her McDonald's uniform. "What about Bert? He's an asshole, like I said, but he's all my mom's got."

"How pissed off was he about Michael Whitby's advances toward you?"

Mandy rolled her eyes. "Oh, like Bert offed this guy! Get real! I'm lucky if Bert gets off the couch long enough for me to watch the 'Real World,' ya know? I mean, he was pissed because he had to be. Mom expected him to be, ya know? But it wasn't like he really gave a big rat's ass one way or another."

"What does Bert do?" I asked. "For a living."

"He works at that tire store over by Wal-Mart. I don't remember the name of it."

"What does he do there?"

Mandy shrugged. "I think he's the manager," she said. "Or something like that."

"What does your mom do?" I asked.

Mandy stood up. "Your ten dollars' worth is up,

lady, 'sides, I gotta get back to work.'' She held out her hand, presumably for the other five. I gave it to her.

"Thanks for your time, Mandy," I said.

She started back to the counter, then turned and looked at me. "Who are you, anyway?" she asked.

I grinned. "If I tell you my name, you might mention it to someone," I said.

She shrugged. "Yeah, probably." She headed for the french fry machine, but stopped. "Oh," she said, turning to look at me. "I just remembered something!"

"What's that?" I asked, my curiosity obviously showing—to my financial regret.

She cut her eyes at me. "It'll cost you another five," she said, grinning.

I pulled out my wallet. I had three dollars and seventy-six cents in cash. I showed it to her. "This is all I've got," I said.

She pocketed the money. "It'll have to do," she said. "One time when Mike came in he had a girl with him."

I felt my skin crawl. "A girl? Who?"

"Her name's Celia something. She's a senior. I don't know her. She's a Mex. We don't hang out in the same crowd, ya know?"

"What do you mean she was with him?"

Mandy rolled her eyes. "*With* him!" she said. "Like she came in with him and they sat down at a table together and he came up here and ordered for both of them. You know, *with* him."

"Celia? A senior this year?" I asked.

"Yeah. Her mom's some bigwig. I don't know

who. Celia's short, got dark, long black hair. You know, typical Mex.''

"You're too young to be a bigot, Mandy,'' I said.

She looked at the money in her hand. "And you're too poor to insult me, bitch. That's all I gotta say.''

With that she went back to her french fries and I gathered the kids and headed home.

Something was bothering me, but I couldn't figure out what. The fact that there was another girl in Whitby's life other than Mandy hadn't surprised me as much as it should have. Why? I suspected there might be others, but it was more than that.

Then it hit me.

I went to my office files where I'd stashed my Xerox copy of Michael Whitby's journal and read through it again.

I found it. October 10. It read, "It wasn't my fault those girls picked on me. It could have been any other guy in the school! And the girls in this town aren't much better. Some of them have already started in. Like that girl at work and the one behind the counter at McDonald's the other night.''

"Like that girl at work.''

Celia?

What was a high school senior doing working with Michael Whitby? This was something I was going to have to find out.

I had way too much on my plate, I decided. Later that night, I gave Willis his share of the burden.

"So you need to go check out this guy Bert,'' I said.

"No," he said, trying to ignore me and read at the same time—a trick he's just not up to accomplishing.

"I think he'd talk easier to a man," I said.

"No," he said.

"Besides the tires on the Ghia aren't looking so hot," I said.

He put the book down. "The tires on the Ghia are fine," he said. "Don't talk bad about the Ghia."

"Well, the tires on the minivan aren't so good."

"They're fine. They're new. Stop it." He picked up his book again.

"Willis, all I'm asking for is a little help. You want to find out who killed Michael Whitby, don't you?"

"Not particularly," he answered, turning a page I knew he hadn't actually read.

"You're not even curious?"

"No," he said.

"You know everybody thinks it was poor Arlene. Even if she's not arrested for it, it'll follow her."

"I don't care."

"So that poor little boy will grow up knowing his father was a pedophile and thinking his mom is a murderer," I said.

Willis sighed and put the book down. "You're good," he said. "Damned good."

I smiled. "Thank you."

"What do you want me to do?" my husband asked.

The next morning I was feeling righteous. Luna picked the kids up for school and I waved them off, not even asking her if she'd looked up the information I'd wanted. Even if she had, she probably wouldn't tell me.

Just like I had no intention of telling her about Celia somebody or even referring her to the mention of a second girl in Whitby's journal. She had the same opportunity I did to follow up on that. We could both play the secrecy game.

Besides, I had Willis going to the tire store to have a little chat with Bert that day, and Carlie interviewing Rene Tillery and Tina Perlmutter. All my balls were in the air and twirling nicely.

Which left me with not only Max Galeana and Davis Perlmutter, but a need to find out a little more about Celia. My best bet was just looking at a high school annual. Codderville High was not terribly large, not even as big as Black Cat Ridge High, and it shouldn't be too hard going through the seniors and finding a girl named Celia. My friend Brenna, my mother-in-law Vera's ward, now a sophomore at Northwestern in Illinois, had graduated from Codderville High two years before. I knew she had a yearbook from her senior year—which would have been when Celia was a sophomore. If she had gone to school at Codderville then. I'd look at Brenna's book first.

I called my mother-in-law and was told in no uncertain terms that today was her hair appointment day and she wouldn't be available for me to go through the stuff in Brenna's room until after school.

"Why don't you bring your little hellions by?" Vera said. "I haven't seen them since you ripped them away from me last week." She stopped for a minute. "Oh, by the way, how you doing?" she asked.

"I'm fine," I said, knowing that in her own way, it was a sincere question. "We won't find out anything more for a couple of weeks."

"Well, ain't medical science wonderful?" she said, making her usual tsk, tsk sound. "They coulda done this back in my day!"

In an unusual display of support for the medical community, I said, "They probably wouldn't have found it back in your day, Vera. At least now they have the machinery for diagnosing this disease."

"Whatever," she said, which is what she says whenever I win an argument. "See you later."

This new plan left me most of the day to deal with Max Galeana and Davis Perlmutter.

The cold snap had broken and the sun was out that day, with the weatherman saying the temperature could rise to the mid-sixties. After a quick breakfast and an even quicker session in my office, trying to get back to the mess I'd made of the life of my heroine, Meg, the parlor maid who didn't know she was actually of royal heritage, and whose illicit longings for Lord Ashton, the dark, dashing, and daring master of the manor, were unrequited—as far as she knew. I was working towards getting them in bed, but my heart wasn't in it. Since I was living a celibate life—by doctor's orders—I didn't see why Meg should be getting any either.

Max Galeana was the Allstate agent for Black Cat Ridge. We had our insurance with an independent agent in Codderville—my mother-in-law's first cousin's daughter's husband's brother—and weren't allowed to change due to family loyalty, but there was no way Max (or Carlie, for that matter) needed to know that.

I drove to the small shopping center where the Food Giant was located, next door to which was Max Galeana's Allstate office. An elderly woman sat at the reception desk when I walked in. She was nearly as old as the secretary I'd picked for Willis, and I couldn't help but wonder if Carlie had had a hand in this lady's employment.

"Hi, honey, can I help you?" the woman said, a big smile on her face.

"I'm looking for Max Galeana. Is he in? I haven't got an appointment, but . . ."

"Oh, honey, that's okay. Just a second. What's your name?"

I told her and she got up stiffly from her desk chair and walked the two steps to the closed door behind her desk. It took longer than you'd think. She knocked briskly, opened the door, and announced me.

The woman made her way back to her desk as Max came out of his office, a big grin on his face.

Max was a very good-looking man. Slight, only about five-foot-nine, with a trim build, he had the dark hair, eyes, and complexion of one of my romance novel heroes. Third-generation Mexican, his straight white teeth gleamed in his dark face, and his eyes sparkled. I had no problem wondering why Carlie had fallen for this guy.

"Hi, E.J.! How you doing?" he asked, leaning forward to kiss me lightly on the cheek.

"Well, mostly great, Max, but I'm having a little problem with my car insurance," I said.

He stretched his arm out towards his office. "Well, you came to the right guy," he said, and followed me inside.

We chatted about rates and benefits and "our needs," Max very carefully writing everything down for me. I took the paper and glanced over it. "This looks great, Max. But I need to talk to Willis—"

"Of course," he said. "I can call him later if you like."

"Let me have him call you after he looks this over."

He started to get up and I said quickly, "So what do you think about all this mess with Michael Whitby?" I was trying for nosy-neighbor nonchalant. He wasn't buying.

Max laughed. "You don't need insurance, do you, E.J.?"

"Of course—" I started.

He waggled his index finger at me, a big grin on his face. "Now, don't lie! Carlie told me what you two girls are up to," he said. "And I think you're here to interrogate me!"

He laughed. Well, he *was* cute. How shallow was I? Shallow enough not to be offended by this condescending son of a gun simply because he was pleasing to the eye? Well, yes.

"Just a few questions," I said, smiling.

He leaned back in his chair, arms behind his head, feet crossed and propped on one of the drawers of his desk. "Okay, shoot," he said. "I mean that figuratively, of course!'' He laughed loudly at his own wit.

''Well, the most important question, of course, is who do you think did this?''

Max shrugged. ''The wife, of course, but Carlie tells me you girls have decided it's not her.''

''No,'' I said, unable to help myself, ''this *girl* doesn't think so.''

''Well, if not the wife, then, I don't know, probably someone we don't even know, E.J. Don't you think?'' he said, frowning and sitting forward earnestly. ''I just know it wasn't anybody in our group! It couldn't be! These people are concerned with *living,* E.J. They're not the type to take a life! You can see that, can't you?''

''I don't think any of us really knows what's in another's heart,'' I said.

''True, true,'' he said, leaning back again. ''But I like to think I'm a pretty good judge of character— you've gotta be in the insurance biz—and I just can't see anybody in our group doing it.'' He shook his head. ''Nope. I'd say it's the father of one of the girls from back where Whitby came from, or maybe somebody he worked with. Have you checked out any of those people?'' he asked.

''Not yet,'' I admitted.

''Well, those people were around him every day. Can you imagine? Having to work with someone when you knew that about them?'' He shook himself and leaned forward again. ''I think what you're doing is just great, E.J., really, and I admire the way Willis just lets you do this, but, me, I'd be worried about Carlie if she got involved, you know what I'm saying?''

He wasn't *that* cute! Willis *letting* me do something, my ass! But I think in his condescending way, Max Galeana was telling me to back off using his wife as Watson to my Sherlock. Well, I figured Carlie could make up her own mind about that!

I stood up. ''Thanks for your time, Max,'' I said.

He walked me out of his office and to the door of the suite. ''If you're really interested in getting a better rate for your car insurance, E.J., talk those figures over with Willis and get back to me. I can make you a hell of a deal. And you know what they say—''

I cringed.

He smiled.

''You're in good hands with Allstate.''

I still wanted a face-to-face with Davis Perlmutter, but I thought it might be a good idea to tackle Abby Dane first. I wasn't finished with her yet. There was still the matter of ''a few things about Davis Perlmutter.'' Better I knew what she was accusing him of before I sat down with him.

Abby Dane worked at the travel agency on the square in Black Cat Ridge. I headed to the heart of Black Cat Ridge, the little square called Black Cat Flats, which housed a too-expensive dress shop; an outrageously expensive sports equipment boutique; Tiffany's Tea Room, for the ladies-who-lunch crowd; a paper store (not newspapers, obviously, and certainly not a stationery store—they would never call it *that* at Black Cat Flats); a store that sold things that you would never actually need in your entire life; and Volner's Travels.

Unlike every other establishment on the square, Volner's was fairly typical of its genre—a long and narrow storefront with two rows of desks—four to a side—with colorful travel posters hanging on the walls.

Abby Dane sat at the second desk on the left, busy on the phone and the computer. She didn't see me when I came in. Another woman did, and asked me with a big smile if she could help me. When I told her I was waiting for Abby, she suggested I browse the rack of package deal brochures by the front door.

I did, not able to make up my mind whether my fantasy vacation was a cruise to Alaska or a week at a spa in Colorado.

Finally Abby got off the phone and the other woman told her of my presence. She started toward me with a big smile, then recognition hit and the smile faded.

She walked toward me rapidly and took my arm. "What do you want?" she hissed.

"We need to talk," I said.

"I told you our conversation was over!" she said, still hissing.

"We can talk about it here, or go have coffee at Tiffany's so no one can overhear us."

"No! Just go away!"

"Do you really want your co-workers knowing you threatened to kill Michael Whitby the day before he was murdered?" I asked, letting my voice grow progressively louder—but not loud enough to be overheard by the other people, most of whom were busy on phones and computers.

Abby pushed me toward the door. "For God's sake!" she hissed. "Go over to Tiffany's. I'll be there in five minutes."

I smiled, gave her a finger wave, and headed out the door. At ten-twenty in the morning Tiffany's Tea Room was fairly empty. The only person sitting at a table eating looked to be one of the employees. I grabbed a table near the window, ordered a latte with hazelnut and whipped cream, and waited.

In about three minutes I saw Abby come out of Volner's and head toward the tea room. She came in, sat down at the table, and glared at me. When the waitress asked her what she wanted, Abby glared at her and said, "Coffee, black."

I could tell the waitress was on the verge of verbalizing the list of coffees to choose from, but one look at Abby's face had her scurrying back to the counter for generic coffee.

I sipped my latte while Abby glared. Finally she said, "What do you want?"

"You were saying something about Davis Perlmutter," I prompted.

Abby threw her head back and her arms up. "My God, you never give up, do you? What was all that shit in my office about me threatening to kill Whitby?"

"Oh, that," I said, dismissing it with a wave of my hand, "we'll get to that later. Right now I want to know about Davis Perlmutter."

Abby leaned forward and hissed at me. "I'm not

supposed to be talking to you! And I don't want to talk to you! Just leave me alone—''

She stopped talking and leaned away as the waitress brought her coffee. Abby glared at the girl and said, "Thank you" in such a way as to make one suspect the sincerity of the statement.

"I'm not telling you jack shit!" Abby said, leaning forward again and again hissing as she spoke.

"Fine. You know my next-door neighbor, don't you? Elena Luna? Homicide detective? I'm not sure if she's heard about you threatening—''

"Just shut up!" Abby hissed, darting glances around the room to see if anyone had heard what I'd said.

"Tell me about Davis Perlmutter," I said.

Abby sighed and hunched her shoulders. "There's nothing to tell," she said dejectedly. "He came on to me once is all. And I hear he does that a lot."

"He's a womanizer?" I asked.

Abby shrugged. "I guess," she said, sipping lethargically at her coffee.

"That's it?" I asked, leaning toward her, glaring myself.

"I didn't say it was anything great!" Abby answered, a distinct whine in her voice. "I just said I knew something about Davis Perlmutter, that's all."

"He came on to you?"

She nodded.

"Verbally or physically?" I asked.

She shrugged. "Both."

"Details," I demanded.

Again Abby sighed and her posture, if possible, got even worse. "He was helping me with my car one day when it wouldn't start. And he, well, you know, sorta patted my butt. And he said he'd take payment out in trade, ha ha. Like that.''

"You think he was just joking?'' I asked.

"It was the kind of statement that you could ignore or flirt back with. I decided to ignore it. He's not my type.''

"Not to mention he's married to your friend and neighbor.''

Abby gave me a look that screamed volumes about my naivete.

"And I've seen him around with some of the other neighborhood women,'' she said.

I shook my head. "I have to get out more,'' I said.

"So I've told you what you wanted to know,'' Abby whined. "Can we forget about everything else?''

"I'm curious as to why you threatened Michael Whitby that Friday,'' I said.

"I didn't threaten!'' she whined. "It was just a suggestion. Everybody was getting so frustrated, you know? I mean, all our vigils and picketing and letter-writing campaign—nothing was working! That creep seemed to be in Black Cat Ridge to stay!''

"So you decided to take matters into your own hands,'' I said.

Abby's eyes got big. "No! For God's sake! You think I killed him?'' She laughed nervously. "Me?'' she squeaked.

"How did the others react when you suggested killing him?''

"It wasn't a *real* suggestion,'' Abby said, the whine very much still in evidence. "It was just frustration, you know? And everybody knew that! They just ignored me!'' Her eyes narrowed. ''Who told you about it anyway? I know Willis wasn't there. It was after the two of you got thrown out!''

''No one responded to your comment? In any way?''

Abby sighed. ''God, I don't remember! They just—ignored me! Really! I can't think of anyone who really responded to what I said! They knew I was just talking, for God's sake!''

''Okay, Abby, tell me this. Eliminating Arlene Whitby, who do *you* think killed Michael Whitby?''

Abby threw up her arms again. ''I don't know! And frankly, E.J., I don't care! Nobody cares except you! Which just goes to prove everything Rene said about you is true!''

I sighed. As usual, I was getting no place, but I was getting there quickly and in great style. I stood up. ''Thanks for your time, Abby. And the latte,'' I said, heading out the door and leaving the check for her.

She called after me. ''E.J.—you're not going to say anything to your neighbor are you? The cop, I mean?''

I shrugged. ''I don't know,'' I said. ''I guess it all depends.''

''On what?'' she whined.

''Whether or not you people piss me off anymore,'' I said, smiled, and headed for the minivan.

Now was the time to talk with Davis Perlmutter. I hadn't been patted on the fanny by a stranger in way too long.

Thirteen

Davis Perlmutter was an engineer at Motorola in Austin and commuted the sixty-something miles every day. I knew this—but I also knew he worked the night shift. Which meant he was at home while his wife Tina was at the high school where she worked as a secretary.

I looked up the Perlmutter's home address and drove over there. It was a much smaller version of Tara—a two-story white colonial with columns and a circular drive. I got out and rang the doorbell and was not surprised to hear the first stanza of "Tara's Theme."

I had to ring the bell twice more before I heard footsteps coming toward me from inside.

Davis Perlmutter peered out at me from the small space he'd opened in the door, the chain still on.

His eyes were bloodshot and he didn't seem to recognize me.

"Davis?" I said, smiling brightly. "E.J. Pugh. Remember me?"

"Who?"

"E.J. We met at Rene Tillery's house—the night of the meeting?"

"Oh, yeah," he said. He smiled sleepily and closed the door and removed the chain, opening it further.

"Sorry, I was asleep. I work nights," he said, which sounded for all the world like an accusation.

"Would it be okay if I came in for a minute, Davis? I really was hoping you could help me with some things," I said, moving briskly past him into a small foyer overpowered by formal black and white checked marble tiles and an antique hall tree the size of a Buick.

"Come in the kitchen while I fix some coffee," he said, taking the lead.

The kitchen was quaint. New appliances masquerading as antiques, very nice faux hardwood floors and counters, and entirely too many things— wreaths, flower arrangements, hanging faux garlic and faux onions, a kitchen witch, etc. Quaint's the word I'm going to stick to.

Davis punched a button on the coffeemaker and it began to gurgle. "Tina makes it for me before she leaves," he said. "All I have to do is hit the button. If I make it myself it tastes nasty." He shrugged. "I don't know why," he said, in that way males the world over have of getting women to do most of the work.

"I bet if you wash clothes everything comes out pink," I said.

He nodded, a look of awe on his face. "Yeah, how'd you know that?" he asked.

Because, I didn't answer, Willis had tried that—once.

The coffee finished brewing and we both fixed cups—his black, mine with Equal and some milk Davis was able to finally unearth in the faux antique "icebox."

We sat down at a small, dainty, faux rosewood table with chairs so delicate I was afraid to put my entire weight on them.

Davis Perlmutter was one of the three guys I was referring to earlier when I said Michael Whitby looked like every third guy in Black Cat Ridge—he was medium height, stocky, had thinning light brown hair, a cherubic face, and watery blue eyes. He was wearing Bugs Bunny shorts and a white T-shirt under a blue terrycloth robe he wasn't able to keep totally closed. He clasped his cup in both hands, elbows on the table, and bent his head to the coffee, slurping long and loud.

Finally he looked up. "Uh, why are you here?" he asked, appearing genuinely puzzled. I figured he and Tina didn't communicate a great deal.

"I'm just really curious about this whole Michael Whitby fiasco," I said.

"Who?" he asked, looking at me with eyes squinched almost shut.

"Michael Whitby?"

"Michael—Oh," he said, nodding his head as

light dawned. "That child molester guy. The one who got killed, right?"

"Right," I said, wondering under what sand dune Davis Perlmutter had his head buried.

"Yeah, my wife and her friend Rene were all up in arms about that," he said. "But he's dead now," he added, looking at me as if imparting information I really needed to know.

"Yes," I said, "I'm aware of that. And I'm trying to figure out who might have killed him."

"Why?" Davis asked, again genuinely puzzled.

Okay, either this guy was a great actor, or he was the *most* self-absorbed person on the face of the earth. I figured it could go either way.

"Don't *you* want to know who killed him?" I asked.

"That Whitby character?" he said. He shrugged. "Not particularly," he said, then yawned. "I figure now maybe Tina will have dinner ready on those few nights I get to be home, ya know? I mean, she was running around with that Rene friend of hers like a crazy woman, trying to do something about the guy. And we've got sons," he said, again genuinely puzzled.

"The one meeting I went to I noticed you were there," I said.

"Yeah, Tina dragged me to one. But I didn't do any of that picketing or stuff 'cause I work nights. Are you a natural redhead?"

I ignored the last comment. "Who do you think killed him?" I asked.

"Because I can tell, you know," he said, "if

you're a natural redhead." He grinned. "It would help, of course, if you were naked."

"Who do you think killed Michael Whitby?" I asked again.

Davis shrugged. "I don't know," he said. He leaned forward, smiling at me. "Who do you think killed him?" he asked.

"Any chance you did it?" I asked. "It would save me a lot of trouble."

He laughed. "Naw," he said, leaning back. "Not my style. Though I thought it might be the neighborly thing to go by and see how the widow's doing," he said, grinning again.

I stood up. "I'd leave Arlene Whitby alone," I said. "Everybody except you thinks of her as their number-one suspect."

He followed me to the door, still grinning, "Hey, I got a trench coat. You wanna play? You be a suspect and I'll be Columbo?"

I left, wondering how he got anywhere with that kind of approach.

When I got home there were several messages on the answering machine. One was from Willis, trying to wiggle out of going to the tire store and speaking with Bert; another was from a local charity letting me know they'd have a pickup truck in the neighborhood on Friday, if I had any usable discards; and one unidentified call—that sounded a great deal like Carlie Galeana, saying simply, "We need to meet. Call me."

I returned the calls in order, assuring my husband that, yes, he still had to go talk to Bert and that I wanted a report as soon as he was through; mentally determining if I had any usable discards and deciding that anything usable I still needed; and then calling Carlie Galeana.

When she answered the phone, I said, in a stage whisper, "Behind the high school gym—midnight!"

"Is that you?" she said.

"If you mean E.J. Pugh, the friendly neighborhood viper, yes it is."

"Rene really has it in for you," she said, her voice low.

"Is she in your living room?" I asked.

"No."

"Then why are you whispering?"

"Because the woman intimidates the hell out of me!" Carlie said, still keeping her voice low. "And if anyone in Black Cat Ridge would own bugging equipment, it would be her!"

"You sure you want to be seen in public with me?" I asked, joking.

"Actually, I was hoping we could meet outside of Black Cat Ridge," she said.

"You've got to be kidding."

"You don't know how bad it is!" Carlie reasoned.

"How bad is it?"

"Pretty damn bad! Meet me at the Hamburger Hut in Codderville for lunch."

"When?"

"One o'clock," she said, her voice low, and hung up.

Someone was going to have to do something about Rene Tillery, and that's all there was to it.

*   *   *

The Hamburger Hut was only about half full at one o'clock. Carlie sat at a booth near the restrooms. I hadn't seen her at first, and had had to walk around the dining room until I found her. Her back was to the door, and the back of the booth was high.

I slid in opposite her. "Aren't you carrying this a little bit far?" I asked.

"Did you know she's starting a petition to have you banned from the Black Cat Elementary PTA?" Carlie whispered, leaning toward me.

I hooted a laugh. "Are you serious? Yea! No more decoration committees! No more bake sales!"

"I *am* serious, E.J.! The woman has more clout than you think!"

I sighed. "Carlie, she can't get me banned from the PTA, more's the pity. Show a little backbone, for crying out loud!"

Carlie shuddered. "She scares me to death, E.J."

"She's a bully. Don't let her intimidate you. What did you find out?"

"Besides the fact that she's starting petitions against you and is working to have Michael, Jr., removed from the school?"

That sobered me up. "She can't do that!" I said.

"One wouldn't think so, would one?" Carlie sighed. "You know she intimidates the principal and every teacher in that damned place!"

"There are rules!" I screeched. "Laws, even! And why would she even care—now?"

"Something about having the child around keeping the 'thought' of the father around, or some such crap!"

"Did you tell her you disagreed with her about this?" I asked.

Carlie looked at the table in front of her and didn't respond.

"If no one ever disagrees with her, Carlie, then she thinks she's won!"

Carlie laughed bitterly. "No, E.J., she *knows* she's won."

I knew I had to make this a quick meeting. I needed to get to Arlene Whitby's house and see what could be done about this—and quickly.

"What else did you find out?"

Carlie sighed. "Not much. You don't interrogate Rene Tillery, E.J. She turns it around on you. I'm afraid she knows how often Max and I have sex and when the last time I farted out loud was."

"What about Tina Perlmutter?"

"What about her?"

"Did you talk with her?"

Carlie shook her head. "Not really. She was there when I talked to Rene." Carlie shook her head again. "Are you sure Tina actually speaks?" she asked. "I'm not sure I've heard her voice."

"Not often at any rate. You've got to get her alone, Carlie. Away from Rene."

Still Carlie shook her head. "I'm not cut out for this crap, E.J."

"Come on," I pleaded—okay, whined. "I need your help here, Carlie."

Carlie looked up with a wistful look on her face. "Wouldn't it be great if Rene did it?" she said. "And we could prove it?"

I laughed. "Yeah, that would be terrific. So talk to Tina."

Carlie sighed. "I don't know—"

"You're the only one who can do it, Carlie," I cajoled.

"But—"

"You know you can," I said.

"But—"

"So let me know what you find out, okay?" I said, getting up from the table.

"E.J.!" Carlie whined.

"Good luck!" I said. Giving her a mock salute, I headed for the door and freedom.

Arlene Whitby's car was in her driveway when I got there. A FOR SALE sign stood in the front yard.

I got out and rang the bell.

The curtain in the door moved slightly then the door opened. Arlene smiled. "E.J.! Hi! Come in!"

I moved into the living room, following Arlene. I'd been in her home before, but under the circumstances I hadn't really checked the place out. This time I did. It looked like a model home designed by an unimaginative decorator with a limited budget.

The living room was furnished with the requisite pieces of furniture, and even a knickknack or two. There was a picture on the wall. There was a flower vase on the coffee table. There were two throw pillows apiece on the couch and loveseat. There was a copy of "Texas Monthly" on a table next to the loveseat. It was a living room.

I sat down on the same couch where I'd sat with Arlene the night we found Michael Whitby's body.

"I see a FOR SALE sign in your yard," I said.

Arlene nodded. "So far all we've gotten are curiosity seekers, but my Realtor thinks I'll be able to sell without too much of a loss."

"Where are you going?" I asked.

"Home," she said. "Back to Tyler where my mother lives. This isn't the place for us."

"I heard there might be some problem at the school about Mikey," I said carefully.

She laughed. "Oh, you mean that Tillery woman and her petition to get Mikey removed from the school? I had my lawyer talk to the principal and, believe me, there'll be no more of that. Besides, with any luck we'll be out of here before Christmas."

I sighed with relief. "I'm sorry about all this, Arlene," I said.

She smiled. "You and your kids have been the only bright light to all of this, E.J. I want to thank you for all you've done." She stood up. "How about some coffee?"

I stood up too. "I'm afraid I need to head for the school shortly to pick up the kids, but thanks."

Impulsively I hugged her. "Call me and let me know what's happening with the move," I said, waved, and headed out the door.

So much for Rene Tillery's clout, I thought. One mention of an attorney and she turned tail and ran. I needed to tell Carlie this. She needed to know Rene wasn't invincible. I used my cell phone to call her, but got only her answering machine. Hoping she was somewhere interrogating Tina Perlmutter, I left a message asking her to call me and hung up.

Then I called Willis as I headed the car toward Black Cat Elementary.

His secretary put me through to him. "What?" he said, not at all graciously.

"Did you talk to Bert?" I asked.

"Would you ever leave me alone if I didn't?" he asked.

"No," I answered.

"Yes, I talked to Bert," he said.

"And?"

"And he wondered who the hell I was and what business it was of mine and where I got my information and who the hell I thought I was."

"Well, those are legitimate questions, honey, but did you get any answers?"

"Other than to fuck off and mind my own business? No, not really."

"Did he abuse you, sweetie?" I asked, in a syrupy voice.

"Sometimes you are not the nicest person in the world, E.J.," my husband said.

"Okay, answer me this: Does he look at all like Davis Perlmutter?" I asked.

Willis laughed. "Not in the least," he answered.

Damn, I thought, there goes that scenario.

"Can I get back to work now?" Willis asked. "Please?"

"So you didn't find out anything?"

"Not for the lack of trying—or the lack of making a fool of myself."

"Okay," I said, "go back to work."

"Thank you," he said. "Goodbye."

I picked up the kids—including Luna's boys—

and headed into Codderville. The boys were totally negative about a trip to ''Grandma's house,'' but the girls, of course, were ecstatic.

Vera was just pulling into the driveway in her ancient Valiant when we pulled up. She got out of the car, her hair curlier and bluer than the last time I'd seen her.

The girls bailed out of the car, screaming, ''Grandma!'' at the tops of their lungs, and lunged into their grandmother's open arms. The boys, however, sauntered nonchalantly out of the van, totally above this nonsense.

''Got fresh-baked chocolate chip cookies in the kitchen,'' she called to the boys.

The nonchalance vanished as the three of them ran, pushing and shoving, for Vera's front door.

Vera took all the kids into the kitchen while I headed for Brenna's old room, hoping the children would leave me at least one or two chocolate chip cookies.

Brenna's room was just as she'd left it when she'd gone back to school in August. And just as it would be for her when she came home again at Thanksgiving. I went to her closet and opened the door, finding the shelves on the side of the closet that Willis had built for her. Most of the books had gone with her to Northwestern, but her outgrown high school yearbooks, a picture album from her life before she came to us, and a few romances (none of mine—she assured me she took those with her to Northwestern to encourage sales) were all that was left on the shelf.

I found Brenna's senior yearbook and opened it to the sophomores. Starting with the ''A's,'' I studied every girl's name, excited when I came to a "Celia." But this one appeared, in the black and white photo, to be a blonde. In the "N's" I found the right Celia. Celia Nunoz—long dark hair, big dark eyes, a heart-shaped face that made her look more like twelve than the fifteen she should have been in the picture. Other than her name, there were a list of her sophomore-year accomplishments: pep squad, FTA (Future Teachers of America), and the swim club. But this was two-year-old stuff. I needed a lot more—like an address and why she was having lunch with Michael Whitby, convicted child molester.

I wrote down the little information I could get and decided that the next day would be the soonest I could get to Codderville High and have a talk with the counselor. I could only hope it was the same one who'd come through for us so well when Brenna transferred to that school.

I gathered up the kids and headed home. When I got there, the answering machine light was blinking again. One message was from Carlie Galeana—she'd call me when she got something, she said. The other message was from Marta Colman's office: "Call the doctor immediately."

The biopsy on the tissue sample from the D&C had been inconclusive. They needed another sample.

"Does that mean another D&C?" I asked.

"No," Marta said. "We can probably do this with just a pelvic. But I want you in here right away. How's tomorrow morning around eight? My usual appointments don't start until nine and I'm through with rounds by about seven-forty-five, so I should be able to squeeze you in then,'' she said.

"Is this bad?'' I asked her.

"No, E.J. It's just what I told you—inconclusive. I'm afraid we didn't get a big enough sample the first time. This will take just a few minutes.''

I sighed. "Okay, I'll be there,'' I said, ever so grateful for yet another pelvic—one of life's little pleasures.

The next morning Willis stayed home to take the kids to school while I headed out for my appointment with Marta Colman. Needless to say, rounds ran long and I'd been lying in the stupid little gown on the examining room table for over half an hour before she showed up.

"I'm sorry, E.J. Couldn't be helped,'' Marta said, coming in snapping on her gloves. "Let's get this done, okay?''

"Ready when you are,'' I said.

"Okay, slide down for me.''

She did her thing while I did my thing—that is, grimace, pant, and leave fingernail prints in my palms.

The nurse took the tissue specimen and headed out the door. I started to get up, but Marta said, "Let's get another blood test while you're here. Check those HCG titers.''

So after all the poking and prodding, I was also punctured, then allowed to dress and be on my way. Willis was still home when I got there.

"Well?'' he said anxiously from the doorway.

I pushed my way into the house. "Honey, what? Like she would know immediately? She has to send the specimen to the lab for a biopsy. This afternoon at the earliest, maybe not even until tomorrow. She also took a blood test to check the HCG level. That has to go to the lab, too.''

"Then I guess I should just go on to work?" he asked. "Or do you want me to stay?"

I pushed him to the door. "Meg's getting laid today," I told him. "She doesn't need a witness."

He kissed me. "Well, as long as someone's getting lucky," he said and headed for the Ghia.

I went into the kitchen and checked my stash of chocolate over the refrigerator. It was getting low. Only a KitKat and one Hersey's Kiss left. I popped the Kiss in my mouth and took the KitKat to the table, knowing I'd have to hit my "supplier" soon. I definitely needed something heavy—like Godiva truffles, or maybe a trip to Austin for Lamm's chocolate-covered strawberries.

I was feeling wounded. I don't like pelvics once a year—and this had been basically my third in as many weeks. And I knew it could get worse. I could be wishing for something as innocent as a pelvic.

I put water on for tea and opened the KitKat. I felt as if my body was betraying me. It had its job to do and I had mine. But, then I thought, looking at the KitKat in my hand, maybe I wasn't being fair. I hadn't been treating my body all that well over the past few years. I was at least twenty-five pounds overweight. I never exercised—except for running up and down stairs to deal with the kids, and although I insisted the kids eat as healthily as possible, I ate junk half the time.

I threw the second half of the KitKat in the trash can.

The phone rang and I picked up, simultaneously removing the KitKat from the trash. "Hello?"

"It's Carlie," she said.

"Hey, what's up?"

"I talked to Tina," she said.

"Great. Do we have to meet some place incognito?" I asked.

Carlie sighed. "No, I know I was being silly. How about coming over here? My turn to pretend to bake something from Food Giant."

I laughed. "I'm on my way."

Carlie lived only two blocks away, but even so I'd never been to her house. It was a one-story ranch with a lot of redwood, white rock, and glass. Two large oak trees shaded the front yard and the driveway led back to a detached garage. I walked up the flagstone walk to a double front door.

Carlie opened on the first knock. "Hey, come on in," she said, leading me toward the kitchen.

I passed a lived-in-looking living room, complete with toys spread across the floor, a worn-looking afghan flung across the seat of an easy chair, and a TV on mute.

Carlie's kitchen was a large, open area with a picnic-style table in the breakfast area and oversized appliances. Like me, Carlie had three children, but she seemed better equipped.

We sat down at the table to coffee cake and weak coffee. "I talked to Arlene Whitby," I told her. "She sicced her attorney on Rene and it appears she's backing off."

I grinned as Carlie sat back in her chair and stared at me. "No kidding?" she said, eyes big. "She's backing off?"

"I don't think even Rene wants to take this to court," I said.

"Well, I can't say I have much respect for Arlene Whitby," Carlie said, grimacing, "but I still have to hand it to her. She's got guts."

"And a good attorney. So what did you find out?" I asked, stuffing my face with the coffee cake—briefly forgetting the "body is temple" promise I'd made myself earlier.

"Not much, really. Davis was at home with the candy dish while Tina was out with their boys. She got them back around nine then went into the den to watch the tube. Neither left all evening."

"Well, that doesn't help," I said, going for a second piece of coffee cake.

"She did talk on the phone with Rene, though," Carlie said.

"Where was Rene?" I asked.

Carlie grinned. "In her car. Or at least on her cell phone, Tina said. She has one of those caller ID things and the phone number that came up she recognized as Rene's cell phone."

I sighed. "I saw her at the Halloween Fest at the school. She was probably coming back from there or taking her girls trick or treating."

"Probably," Carlie agreed.

I sighed again. "Why do I feel like we're exactly where we were the day Whitby got killed?"

"Because we are," Carlie said, heading for her second piece of coffee cake. "I know you've done

this before, E.J.—this snooping around in murder—
how do you stay interested? I mean, this is getting
boring!''

"Because there's usually something happening at
this point,'' I told her. Then I thought back—oh,
yeah, usually something happening: like people
breaking into my house, being accosted in churches
with guns, being held captive at a turkey farm—fun
things like that. "But maybe it's best,'' I said, "that
nothing much is happening.''

"Doesn't that mean we're not getting very close
to the killer?'' she said. "I mean, on 'Murder She
Wrote,' if Jessica gets close to the killer, then something bad happens.''

"That's fiction,'' I said, then relayed to her my
own theory on Jessica Fletcher: that she was one of
the greatest serial killers in the history of the United
States, able to convince other people they'd commit-
ted the crimes, and she'd been getting away with
this for years—even into reruns.

Carlie laughed. "You're right—I'd never let that
woman in my house. She visits, you know somebody's going to die.''

"Exactly my point,'' I said.

"Let's hope you don't get like that,'' Carlie said.

"You notice I rarely leave Black Cat Ridge,''
I said.

Carlie frowned. "Point taken,'' she said.

I left Carlie's and headed for Codderville. It was
time for a talk with the high school counselor.

Inez Peabody was in her sixties, had steel-gray
helmet hair, reading glasses on a rhinestone-studded
strap hanging around her neck, wore sensible shoes,

a matching sweater set that had been very chic in the early sixties, and a brown tweed skirt that reached her mid-calf. I'm sure that someone walking down any street in America, upon seeing Inez Peabody walking toward them, would say to themselves, "Schoolteacher." And they'd be right, but, strangely enough, she's one of the few in the Codderville Independent School District that look like that. The majority, although mostly female, run to mid-thirties, with at least two children attending school in the district, and came equipped with husbands who make salaries high enough for their wives to afford to be schoolteachers.

Inez Peabody was an exception—in age, dress, marital status, and income. She was an old maid schoolteacher living on the small income that provided in a small house in Codderville. She was also one of the nicest, most no-nonsense, let's-get-the-job-done-and-done-right types I'd met in my lifetime. After all her help with Brenna a few years before, I'd have walked barefoot on broken glass if Inez Peabody asked me to do so.

She was in her office and broke into a broad smile when I knocked on her door, peeking my head around.

"Well, E.J., you thing! Get on in here!" she said, standing up to hug me. "How's Brenna?" she asked, as she always did.

"Got a B last semester in chemistry and it almost killed her."

"I take it she's still planning on summa cum laude?" Inez asked.

"Right before the Nobel Prize," I said, grinning.

"Sit, sit," Inez said, heading back behind her desk. "I know you're up to something or you wouldn't be here—"

"That's not true—"

She grinned. "Yes it is. What's up?"

"Celia Nunoz," I said.

Inez cocked her head. "She's one of my students, yes."

"What can you tell me about her?" I asked.

Inez leaned back in her chair. "Absolutely nothing without her and her parents' permission," she said.

"You've been reading about Michael Whitby and all the to-do in Black Cat Ridge, I take it?"

Inez grimaced. "The man's dead, E.J. All I can do is thank Providence for that. I know I shouldn't, but I can't help myself."

I nodded. "Most people feel that way, Inez. I guess it's pretty normal."

"What has that horrible man to do with Celia Nunoz?"

I explained Michael Whitby's journal entries, leaving out Mandy Hogkins's name, and how I got to Celia Nunoz's name.

"Celia was having lunch with that man?" Inez asked, her eyes huge. "Oh, my goodness. This is not good. Oh, my goodness."

"I've wondered about Michael Whitby's MO," I said. "How he operated. I haven't, of course, been able to get the police to tell me anything, but I wondered if, back in East Texas, he went after one girl at a time, or if he'd have two on a string, or what. Which made me wonder if there was someone else other than the girl I mentioned. Then I found out about Celia. I'm worried that he might already have, well . . ."

"Been up to his old tricks with Celia?" Inez asked.

I nodded my head.

The look on Inez's face made me realize how lucky I was to be her friend—and not her enemy. She stood up. "I'll get Celia out of class now. You stay here. We'll talk to her together."

"What about her parents?" I asked.

"Just follow my lead. I'll ask the questions. I know how far I can go without parental permission. You just be quiet."

"Yes, ma'am," I said, as she headed out the door.

Celia Nunoz had aged a little since her sophomore picture had been taken for the yearbook. Now instead of twelve she looked at least fourteen. She was a tiny girl, no more than five foot, and very slender, although she had quite impressive breasts—impressive enough to make me wonder how she was able to stand upright.

She came in Inez's office smiling, but the smile faded when she saw me, a stranger, sitting there.

The girl cocked her head at Inez, who made quick introductions.

"Celia, please, have a seat," Inez said, taking her chair behind the desk. "Ordinarily I would never think of prying into your personal business, but, unfortunately, we have some extraordinary circumstances right now. If you feel uncomfortable with any of my questions, I want you to let me know and we'll call your mother immediately and she can sit in on this discussion.''

Celia looked from her counselor to me and back again. "What's this about?" she asked.

Inez took a deep breath. "Are you familiar with a man named Michael Whitby?"

Celia's olive complexion turned a dark red. She shrugged her shoulders but didn't answer Inez's question.

"You've heard the name?" Inez persisted.

Celia nodded her head.

"Did you ever meet him?"

The girl, head bent, mumbled something under her breath that neither Inez nor I heard.

"Please speak up, dear, I didn't understand you," Inez said.

The girl sighed. "He worked in the building where I'm interning," she said.

Inez leafed through a file on her desk. "Oh, yes. You're interning with the city water department this semester, right? That would be at the municipal building?"

Celia nodded.

"He worked for the parks department," I said.

Celia looked at me, then quickly looked away. Inez also looked at me—but her look said firmly and with no equivocation that I should keep my mouth shut.

Inez clasped her hands in front of her on top of her desk and leaned forward, an earnest look on her face. "Celia, dear, I don't want to pry, but if there's anything you need to talk about, I'm here for you."

Celia glanced at me again. "I didn't know who

he was when I went to lunch with him," she said. "I swear! I never would have gone, believe me!"

"Was he in any way ungentlemanly with you, dear?" Inez asked.

Celia shook her head. "No, not at all. At first. I mean, when I went out to lunch with him, but then he kept coming by my office all the time and one of the women there told me who he was and she moved me to another desk so he wouldn't come by anymore."

"Did he stop?" I asked.

Inez shot me a look.

"Sorry," I said.

"You may answer her question if you wish," Inez said to Celia, "but you don't have to, of course."

"Yeah, he stopped coming by," she said, then ducked her head again. "But then he started calling me."

"At work?" Inez asked.

Celia nodded. "And at home," she added.

Inez took a deep breath. "Did he touch you, Celia?" she asked.

Celia shook her head, unable to look up. "No. I told my mother and she told my uncle and then he just stopped calling."

"When was this?" I asked.

Celia looked at me. "Huh?"

"When did he stop calling?" I asked.

She shrugged. "I dunno. I guess, well, like a week or two ago."

"How soon before he was killed?" I asked.

Celia's eyes got big. "I didn't kill him!" She stood up and looked at Inez, panic in her eyes.

"Gawd, Miss Peabody! You don't think I killed him—"

Inez stood. "No, dear, of course not." She glared at me. "Ms. Pugh, would you mind waiting outside?"

I got up and left, knowing I'd stepped in it this time. I just hoped the good relationship I'd had with Inez Peabody could weather this.

I sat in a chair outside Inez's office for another ten minutes. Finally, the door opened and Celia Nunoz came out, Inez right behind her.

"Come back any time, dear," Inez said with a smile. "We'll talk."

Impulsively, Celia hugged Inez, then turned red again. "Thanks, Miss Peabody," she said, stole a glance my way, then headed back to class.

Inez looked at me. I felt I was back in junior high and I'd just been caught letting the cute boy in the row next to mine cheat off my homework.

She nodded her head towards her office and went inside. I followed, taking the seat I'd been expelled from earlier.

Inez tapped her fingers on her desktop, giving me a look. She was very good at this.

"I'm sorry," I said.

Still, I got the silent treatment.

"Really," I said. "I'm sorry. Really sorry."

"You upset the girl," Inez said, her voice steady, tone moderate.

I hung my head. "I know. I apologize."

"I'm not the one you should be apologizing to."

"I wouldn't think you'd want me speaking to her again."

"I don't," Inez said, straightening up and picking up Celia Nunoz's file to put away. "I hope you got what you wanted," she said, standing.

I stood too. "I'm sorry, Inez. I get carried away sometimes."

She smiled. "If you didn't get carried away, my dear, little Brenna would be spending some not-so-quality time in juvenile hall, more than likely."

She put her arm around me and led me to the door. "But still and all, I said to follow my lead."

I lowered my head. "I know," I said. "I'm sorry."

"Let's just see that it doesn't happen again," she said, smiled sweetly and shut the door in my face.

I took a deep breath and left the school, thankful I hadn't had to spend any time in the principal's office.

I headed home, tail figuratively between my legs. I passed Friar Tuck Lane, the street where Arlene Whitby lived, and saw her FOR SALE sign in the front yard. I marveled at the way she'd handled Rene Tillery and Rene's campaign to oust Mikey from Black Cat Elementary. Actually, that was quite un-Arlene-like. She'd actually taken charge of the situation and done something about it. *And* she'd put her house up for sale and was prepared to move all by herself. Another uncharacteristic thing.

Everyone kept saying, "It had to be the wife. The spouse is usually the one." And I kept saying, "No way. Not Arlene Whitby—she doesn't have the gumption.'' Well, maybe I was wrong. She had the gumption to take on Rene Tillery, when most people, including myself, shied away from that. She was definitely getting her act together.

Was this because of the release of her husband's death? The weight of the man's baggage being lifted from her shoulders? More than likely. But was that just a result of his death—or a plan on her part? Starting with his murder?

I shook my head. Not Arlene, I told myself. It just didn't make sense.

I pulled into my driveway and got out of the car, determined to head to my office and get Meg laid.

Fourteen

Well, I'm proud to say it happened. Meg was deflowered. Unlike most virgins, she seemed to know precisely what to do and where everything went, and, of course, she was able to achieve multiple orgasm, a feat accomplished by most women, virgins or not, only in the pages of romantic fiction, I'm sorry to say.

After that it was time to pick up the kids and start dinner. And they say my life isn't exciting.

I tried not to think about the new biopsy and if Dr. Colman had been entirely truthful with me. Somewhere deep in my belly I knew the second biopsy was not a good thing. I popped another pill to keep down my lunch, and tried to think of something else.

Like who killed Michael Whitby. I can't say it

was my most honest investigation, but it helped. I knew who I was doing it for—certainly not Michael Whitby, and, in reality, not even Arlene and Mikey; I was doing it for me.

But I consoled myself with the thought that often good things come from selfish reasons. When I tried to enumerate said things, I decided to move on to something else.

The way Arlene Whitby had handled the school problem brought on by Rene Tillery made me wonder if maybe she *was* devious enough to have killed her husband and planted his body on her own front porch—making it look as though she couldn't have been stupid enough to have done it that way.

But then what was devious about hiring an attorney? I suppose I would have done the same thing under similar circumstances. It wasn't as though Arlene herself had done anything—she'd gotten a hired gun to do it.

But then I had to remember that Arlene was the one who "found" Michael Whitby's journal. Wasn't that interesting? It just *happened* to be in his car which just *happened* to still be at his office. And the night watchman just *happened* to call her about it.

Of course, on the other hand, it made perfect sense.

But then on the third hand—and, boy, sometimes did I wish I was so equipped—Michael Whitby *did* threaten to kill Arlene in the pages of that journal that she just *happened* to find.

Then, of course, there was all this new information about Celia Nunoz. Celia said she'd told her mother. And that her mother had told her uncle. And all this was, presumably, before Michael Whitby had been killed. Now, if I'd just had carte blanche to question Celia a little more—But certainly not anywhere near Inez Peabody. If Inez discovered I talked to the girl on my own I had a feeling she would very cheerfully and adroitly dismember my body parts and store them where they'd never be found.

I decided to concentrate on dinner and leave detecting, as well as medicine, to the experts.

I turned on the TV in the family room to the local news, a little noise to cook by. I wasn't paying too much attention until I heard the newswoman say, "And in a related incident in Codderville, school board president Lydia Galeana Nunoz said today that the board will be looking into alleged wrongdoing on the part of the superintendent's aides . . ."

I stopped what I was doing and stared at the TV. There she was: Lydia Galeana Nunoz, school board president for the Codderville Independent School District, standing on the steps of the school district administration building, reading a prepared statement to the press. Funny, but her daughter was the spitting image of her. And both bore a striking resemblance to Max Galeana.

"So then he goes, 'Your daddy was a bad man and he deserved to die!' and Michael goes, 'Take it back!' and Timothy goes, 'Will not!' and Michael hits him right in the mouth!"

"This wouldn't be Timothy Perlmutter?" I asked Megan who stood in front of me in the living room, hands on hips, regaling me with that day's school exploits.

"Yeah, you know him, Mama?" she asked, impressed.

"I know his mother," I said. "How badly was he hurt?"

"Oh, he started bleeding and everything!" my darling daughter said, a big grin on her face. "It was cool!"

I shook my head, wondering about the repercussions of this incident. Arlene needed to get Michael, Jr., some therapy and be damn quick about it. But with her strong fundamentalist beliefs I was afraid she wouldn't. Maybe her preacher would be enough, but even as I thought it I doubted he was equipped for the kinds of problems Michael Whitby, Jr., was going to have.

"Michael shouldn't have hit him," I told my daughter.

Megan rolled her eyes. "Gawd, Mom! He deserved it!"

"We've talked before about how violence never solves a problem—it just causes more problems," I said, mother-cap firmly in place.

I was afraid Megan was going to lose an eye—the way they were both rolling around in her head. "Mother!" She stomped a foot. "Sometimes it's the only answer!" she said.

"That's not true," I countered.

"Well, Mother, you weren't there," she said. "So I don't see how you can know!"

With that, she turned and walked off. I was shocked and a little bit proud, thinking my baby was old enough now to have her own opinions—and fight for them. Proud and, truth be known, pretty damned sad.

But my problem wasn't Timothy Perlmutter and Michael Whitby, Jr.; it wasn't even my daughter's firm opinions on the use of violence. My problem was I wasn't getting any answers. And the reason I wasn't getting answers was because I didn't have any leverage. The only real answers I'd gotten were from Abby Dane—and that was because I'd had leverage.

I considered Bert still a fine suspect; Willis had gotten nothing from him, and I had to wonder why. Okay, here was this stranger asking very personal questions, but still . . .

What kind of leverage could I get on Mandy's Bert? Why not the same thing I'd used on Abby? The threat on Michael Whitby's life. Bert may not have said those exact words, but the message was certainly implied.

And then there was what I'd learned earlier about Celia Nunoz. Mandy had mentioned Celia's mother was a "bigwig." Well, president of the Codderville school board was a pretty big wig all right. And Celia said she told her mother about Michael Whitby's attentions and her mother had told her uncle. Almost immediately the attentions stopped. And Michael Whitby was murdered.

Galeana wasn't a common name. There was a striking physical resemblance between Lydia Galeana Nunoz and Max Galeana. I'd bet the grocery money on the fact that Max Galeana was Celia Nunoz's uncle. And Max had not been forthright with me. Not at all.

Maybe Carlie Galeana had been right not to just naturally assume her husband's innocence. I thought that the next day, along with having a chat with Mandy's Bert, I might take a closer look at my insurance.

I went to bed that night with a smile on my face. I had a plan.

It was the Firestone tire store, less than a block from Wal-Mart. It was the first time I'd been in there since they'd refused to honor a warranty on the tires on my old station wagon two years before. I'd always meant to write a letter about that.

I looked for the person who looked the least like Davis Perlmutter and found him in a glassed-in office with a sign on the door that said, "Bert Pumphries, Manager." Okay, that was cheating a little, but he really didn't look a bit like Davis Perlmutter.

He was maybe thirty at the most, and someone sometime had told him he resembled the king of rock and roll. His dark hair was in a tall pompadour with a spit curl hanging over his forehead, and he actually wore the collar of his Firestone workshirt up in the back. There was what appeared to be a pack of cigarettes tucked into the sleeve of the shirt, and if his jeans had been any tighter he could give up any thought of ever siring children.

He had full lips, big, dark, smoldering eyes, and a strong chin. If his ears hadn't stuck out like Alfred E. Newman's, he would have been the spitting image of Elvis.

Until he spoke.

When I went to his office door and knocked, he

said, "Come in," and I was reminded strongly of another late legend—this one of the writing field—Truman Capote. It was a high, small, squeak of a voice. I could only hope that when Bert did his Elvis imitations late at night he lip-synched.

"Mr. Pumphries?" I asked.

"Yes, ma'am?" he said, standing up behind his desk, just like Elvis's mama would have taught him.

"I wonder if I could have a few minutes of your time?" I asked.

"Sorry, ma'am, but there ain't no solicitin' allowed on the premises," he said. I assumed he thought I was selling something other than my flesh.

"I'm not selling anything, Mr. Pumphries," I said. "I'm a friend of Mandy's. And we have to talk." I shut the door behind me and took a seat in the chair in front of his desk.

Bert sat, frowning at me. "What's this about, ma'am?" he asked.

"It's about Michael Whitby," I said.

The frown deepened. "I don't know what you're talking about, ma'am, and I'm pretty busy." He stood up. "I'm afraid you're gonna have to leave, ma'am."

I stayed seated. "I'm associated with the police, Mr. Pumphries, although I have not yet told them of your involvement with Michael Whitby."

He laughed. "My what? Lady, I already talked to the police. And to Mandy. I think you're that lady that paid her the ten bucks to tell where I worked, huh? And then some man shows up here giving me grief. Lady, I really think you need to leave."

I stayed my ground. "I just have a couple of questions for you, Mr. Pumphries," I said.

"And I ain't got even one answer for you, so I think maybe you should just leave."

I didn't budge. "You seem like a nice man, Mr. Pumphries," I said. "Not the type to bodily throw a woman out of your office. And I hate to tell you, but that's the only way you're getting me out of here until I get answers."

Bert sighed and sat down. "What *is* your problem, lady?"

"I know part of what happened with Michael Whitby from Mandy, but I'd like the rest of the story from you."

He raised his hands in a sign of surrender, a very Elvis-like sneer on his lips. "I swear, ma'am, there wasn't nothing to it. Can't even remember the details."

I settled back in the chair. "Then I hope you're prepared for me to move in here," I replied, smiling.

He smiled back. "Now, ma'am, don't make me call the police."

"Elena Luna, 555-7443, extension 211. She's the detective in charge. Oh, and my best friend." I pushed his desk phone toward him, fairly secure in my bluff. "Tell her I said hey."

He pushed the phone back. "What is it you want?" he asked, the Elvis sneer a thing of memory.

"I want the details of what happened with Michael Whitby."

"Shit," he said, then leaned back in his chair and glared at me. "Who was that man who came to see me?" he asked.

"My husband," I said.

"His heart sure wasn't in it," he said.

"I'm not surprised. On the other hand, I'm here with not only my whole heart, but my liver and spleen to boot."

"I suppose that means something," he said.

"It means I'm not leaving until you tell me what I want to know."

He sighed and leaned forward. "Look, lady, I didn't even know who the fucker was when he showed up with Mandy, ya know? I mean, here's this old coot driving Mandy home from work and Cathy—that's Mandy's mother—she goes, 'Bert, there's somebody in that car out there giving Mandy grief,' and I say, 'Well, she got in the car with 'em,' and Cathy goes, 'You go out there now and you deal with that, you hear me?'" Bert made a face and leaned back. "Well, you know women," he said, then laughed. "Well, I guess you do! You being one and all!"

"So you went out there?"

"Yeah, and this old coot was groping Mandy big time. And I could tell the girl wasn't having any of it, cause she was pushing at him and she wasn't smiling. You know, when a woman pushes at you, sometimes she smiles when she does it and you know that it's really okay. But Mandy wasn't smiling and I didn't like the look of this sucker, not to mention he was old enough to be her daddy and then some. So I pulled open the door on the driver's side and yanked the jackass by his shirt collar right out of the car. He fell on the ground, sputtering and blathering. I told Mandy to get on in the house and

I told him he ever comes near the girl again, I'm gonna make dog food outta his ass. He said something dumb like, 'Oh, yeah?' and I said, 'Yeah.' Then he gets in his car and drives off. And lady, that's it.''

"Did you know who he was?"

He shook his head. "Ma'am, I didn't know shit until he got hisself murdered and I saw his picture in the paper. Then I remembered reading something about all the mess about him being a jailbird and how you high-faluting types up in Black Cat Ridge don't take to jailbirds.'' He shook his head again. "That's all I know. Honest.''

"He wasn't just a jailbird, Mr. Pumphries. He was a pedophile.''

"Uh-huh," he said, a frown on his face.

"A child molester. He liked teenaged girls."

"Well, now, I think I may a read about that. But sometimes, ya know, teenaged girls, they're just asking for it."

"It's against the law," I said, trying not to grit my teeth.

"True, true," he said, standing up and heading for the door. "Now, like I said, that's all I can tell you. That was the only time I ever seen the man, and like I said, I really didn't care one way or the other. Cathy just got her mama-juices going, you know what I mean?"

"Did Whitby call the house after that?"

Bert shrugged. "Not my house," he said. "I don't answer the phone."

Finally, I stood up. "Thank you for your time, Mr. Pumphries."

He laughed. "Well, ma'am, ordinarily I'd say you're welcome, but I'm afraid that might just encourage you to come back, ya know?"

I drove away wishing Bert Pumphries had told me something. Anything that would have moved me from where I was. Because I seemed to be stuck right smack dab on square one. If what he'd said was true, and at this point I had no real reason to doubt him, Bert hadn't even known who the man was who had been harassing Mandy. And the way it sounded, he really didn't care—just going through the motions for the sake of his girlfriend.

I pulled into the parking lot of the Food Giant and pulled into a space in front of Max Galeana's Allstate office. The same elderly woman sat at the front desk, staring blankly at a computer screen.

She smiled when she saw me. "Hello," she said. "May I help you?"

"I wonder if I could speak with Max for a moment," I asked.

Her smile dipped into a frown. "I'm sorry, but Mr. Galeana's out of town today. Actually, he may be gone tomorrow, too." She grabbed a pen and a "while you were out" slip. "May I have him call you?"

I gave her my name and number and left, heading home.

I pulled into the driveway and went in the house. The answering machine was blinking again—this time only once. The message was simple: "E.J., it's Marta Colman. Call me when you get in."

I dialed her number with my purse and car keys

still in my hand, my jacket still on. Naturally, Dr. Colman was with a patient and unable to come to the phone, but the receptionist said she'd have her call me back.

I didn't like it. I was in a waiting game within a waiting game within a waiting game. I didn't seem to *own* anything. Not even my own time.

I put down my purse and car keys, took off my jacket, and put the kettle on to boil. Checking the stash over the refrigerator I discovered I was completely out of chocolate—an occurrence that hadn't happened to my knowledge in at least a year.

My hands started to shake and I shut the cabinet door quickly, consoling myself that I really didn't have that bad a "jones." I could live without chocolate for a few hours—until I left to pick the kids up. Really. I could do it.

The water boiled and I fixed myself some tea, using real sugar instead of Equal, and considered trading in my chocolate habit for cigarettes. Somehow, that seemed contradictory to my "body is temple" ambitions.

The phone rang and I jumped about a foot. I let it ring a second time then picked it up.

"Hello?"

"E.J., hi, it's Marta Colman," she said.

"Yes?"

"Hon, you okay?"

"You tell me," I said, my voice guarded.

"Well, the biopsy came back negative, which is good. Unfortunately, the HCG hormone levels are still high—but basically at the same levels. They haven't gone up, which is also good. The only thing

I can propose we do at this point is wait out the rest of the three-week period and test the levels again.''

"They haven't gone down at all?" I asked.

"Not yet, but that's not to say they won't, E.J. We still have time. And like I said, even if it is malignant—"

"My chances are very, very good," I said, voice on cruise-control.

Marta sighed. "We're okay at this point, E.J."

"Uh-huh," I said.

"See you at your next appointment."

I roused myself. "Thanks for calling, Marta."

"Hang in there," she said and hung up.

I was antsy, fidgety, and anxious. And I knew what I needed to help me over the hump. Chocolate would be nice—but a fight would be better.

I got in the van and headed for Rene Tillery's house. I figured who better to fight it out with than the woman in charge?

My frustrations grew worse. Rene wasn't home. Her car wasn't in the driveway and no one answered the doorbell when I rang.

Tina Perlmutter wouldn't exactly be a fair fight, I thought, but at least it would be better than sitting at home waiting.

I got in the van and drove to Tina's, punching the doorbell and listening once again to the sounds of "Tara's Theme."

The door opened and Tina Perlmutter stood there with her mouth open, staring at me.

I smiled. "Hi, Tina! May I come in?" I asked, not bothering to wait for an answer.

"Ah, E.J., ah, hi, ah . . ." Tina sputtered.

"Can we talk?" I said, sounding for all the world like Joan Rivers and enjoying every minute of Tina Perlmutter's discomfort.

I crossed the overly formal black and white tiled foyer and moved into the living room, crowded with way too much ornate, antique furniture for the size, and sat down gingerly on a red velvet settee.

Tina sat on the edge of a brocade-covered rocking chair, hands in her lap. "What is it you want, E.J.?" she asked, her eyes shifting around the room, as if afraid Rene Tillery would show up any minute and accuse her of high treason.

"We need to talk, Tina."

"About what?" she said, shifting on the tiny space of rocking chair her butt was covering.

"So many things," I said, smiling. "Like your mothering skills for one."

Tina turned pale. "What?"

"According to reliable sources, your son told Michael Whitby's son that his father deserved to die. Now, even if that is how you feel, what kind of mother would convey such a thing to a nine-year-old child?"

Tina stood up. "You better leave," she said. Her voice, her body, everything shook.

"No, not yet. I can't help but think that anyone with mothering skills that poor might also have poor impulse control. So, what exactly were you doing on Halloween? The night Whitby was killed? I'd like a play by play, if you don't mind, say, starting at seven?"

"Leave," she said.

I shook my head and smiled. "Not going to happen," I said. "You see, I'm pissed. Not really at you, and I'm sorry about that, but I feel a need to strike out and, well, Tina, you're handy. So, I want to know what you were doing, and what Davis was doing, and how the two of you think you're going to get away with killing Michael Whitby."

Tina sank back to the brocade-covered rocking chair, her face even whiter than it had been. "We didn't," she said, her voice barely above a whisper. "I mean, no, we didn't. I didn't! And I know Davis didn't! God, what are you saying?"

"Somebody did it, Tina. You'll agree with that, won't you?"

Tina nodded. "Of course, somebody—but not us!"

"Then who?"

"Huh?"

"Who did it?" I asked, my voice hard, leaning toward her.

She leaned back. "I don't know!" she said, arms crossed over her chest, legs pulled up under the rocking chair.

"Yes you do," I said.

Her eyes got big. "No I don't!" she said.

I just looked at her. "Where were you Halloween?"

"I took the kids trick or treating! Honest! I even went up to some houses with them! Check with Dorothy Mason! You know her, don't you? I went up to speak with her when the kids went up! I swear, she'll verify that I was there."

"What time was that?"

Tina looked about her, panic in her eyes. "Uh, I . . . I don't know. I don't know!" she wailed.

"What about Rene?" I asked.

"Huh?"

"Where was Rene on Halloween?"

"I don't know!"

"Carlie Galeana said you got a phone call from Rene."

"Yes. Yes I did," Tina said eagerly.

"Where was she?" I asked.

"I don't know. But she was on her cell phone!" Tina said, obviously eager to get the eye of the inquisitor off of her and her husband and on to Rene. Ah, loyalty. Where did it go?

"How do you know she was on her cell phone?"

"Because I have caller ID and it was that number that came up."

"Where was she?"

"I don't know! She didn't say. I swear, E.J., she didn't say where she was!"

"And you didn't ask?" I demanded.

Tina gave me a look. "Ask Rene where she was?" She laughed nervously. "Well, no, I'd never do that," she said.

Boy, was Tina whupped or what?

"Where do you think she was?" I asked.

Tina looked panicked. "I don't know! Really, I have no idea! You don't think—" she started eagerly, then the doorbell let out with another blast of "Tara's Theme."

Tina looked toward the foyer, then at me, then at the foyer, then at me. Finally she got up and stared at the foyer. Then she looked at me. Taking tiny steps, she headed towards the front door.

I heard it open, heard Rene Tillery's voice, "Well, it's about time you opened the door, Tina! What *were* you doing? Well, never mind, we've got a lot to do—"

"She's in there accusing you!" Tina said loudly.

I stood up and faced the foyer. Rene might play a lot of tennis, but I had bulk on my side.

Rene stepped into the living room. I thought I heard the first stanza of the theme from "The Good, the Bad, and the Ugly," but maybe it was just in my head.

"Well, E.J.," Rene said, smiling. "It's been a while."

I smiled back. "Hasn't it?" I said. "How are you, Rene?"

She moved further into the room. "Never better," she said, the smile still firmly in place. Tina hunkered behind her.

"Tina's been telling me some very interesting things," I said, smiling.

Rene's smile wavered, but remained. Behind her, Tina said, "I have not!"

Rene reached a Nike-clad foot behind her and nudged Tina, who immediately shut up. "You seem to be causing as much trouble as ever, E.J.," she said, the smile still in place.

I sat back down on the settee. Smiling back, I said, "I try."

Rene laughed and took Tina's former place on the brocade rocking chair. Tina remained standing, to the side and behind her leader.

"Well, it's nice of you to drop by and see Tina, E.J., although I doubt you were invited for a coffee klatch."

We both laughed. "Oh, no, not me!" I said.

"I mean, who would want you in their home for a social visit?" Rene said, and we both laughed again.

"Not anyone in your vigilante group!" We were both laughing so hard we were about to slap our knees.

"Well," Rene said, smiling and standing, "get the hell out, E.J." The smile faded. "Nobody wants you around."

"Now that's not true," I said, standing, *my* smile still firmly in place. "Tina and I were having a wonderful chat. Trying to figure out where you were on Halloween—the night Michael Whitby was shot—you know, when you called her on your cell phone?"

Rene's facial muscles twitched in her need to turn an accusing face toward Tina, but, I'll give her this, she remained ever vigilant. "Tina," she said, never removing her eyes from me, "why don't you show your guest to the door?"

Tina jumped and let out a little yelp when Rene said her name, then gathered her strength and headed for the door, no doubt hoping I'd follow.

I decided to do just that. I'd had about as much fun as I could stand.

Fifteen

My trip to Tina Perlmutter's house had accomplished little more than assuring me the title of "the least-liked woman in Black Cat Ridge." But I'd had fun. I'll admit it.

I knew I was getting nowhere. What good was asking people what their alibis were for that night when I had no way of proving or disproving what they said? Now, if I could just get Elena Luna to tell me what she knew—which was about as likely as having Rene Tillery nominate me for Black Cat Elementary Mother of the Year.

I couldn't get my hands on Max Galeana, at least not until the next day, or even the day after that. I couldn't talk to Celia Nunoz without repercussions from Inez Peabody. But nobody said I couldn't talk to Celia's mother—the president of the Codderville school board.

I drove into Codderville to the school district administration office. I knew school board president was an unpaid position and doubted if I'd find Lydia Galeana Nunoz there in the middle of a weekday, but I hoped someone might be able to tell me where I could find her.

I went into the administration office and was greeted by a woman who would have no problem taking on the role of Nurse Ratchet if they ever do a remake of *One Flew Over the Cuckoo's Nest.*

She stood to meet me when I ambled up to the chest-high counter, and smiled. Sort of. One side of her lips twitched upward for a split second. I had to assume it was meant as a smile.

"Help you?" she said, her words clipped.

"Yes, I'm looking for Lydia Galeana Nunoz. I know she's probably—"

"Not in."

"Yes, I figured that. I was wondering if you could tell me—"

"Wednesdays. Four to six."

She turned and headed back to a desk in the bullpen behind the counter.

"Ah, excuse me. Ma'am?"

She turned. She raised an eyebrow.

"I was hoping you could tell me where I could find her now."

"No."

She turned and took a seat behind the desk, picking up a ringing phone simultaneously.

There was no one else behind the counter.

I sighed and headed for the hallway.

A man called to me as I started toward the front door.

"Lady, you looking for Miz Lydia?" he asked.

He was a short Latino, dressed in blue work pants and a blue work shirt with "Jesus" stitched on the pocket of the shirt. He was slightly stooped, with graying hair and the straightest, whitest, phoniest-looking teeth I'd ever seen. He held a broom in one hand and an unlit cigar in the other.

"Yes, sir," I said. "Can you help me?"

"Miz Lydia, she comes in here some, more than just on Wednesday like old Anita tole you. She have a office here," he said, pointing down the hall. I looked in that direction, just as he said, "But she ain't here now. Just sometime she come in. Usually, though, she be at her shop."

"What shop?" I asked.

"Lydia's Imports over by the Wal-Mart. On Jackson?"

I nodded. I'd passed the place but never been in.

"Thanks, Jesus," I said. "I appreciate your help."

"No problem," he said, grinning a beautiful grin full of phony teeth. "That Anita, she don't like to help nobody."

I laughed. "I got that impression."

"You ever need to know anything around here, Mrs., you come ask Jesus, okay?"

"Okay," I said, waved and headed for the front door.

Lydia's Imports was filled to the brim with Mexican bowls, statuary, lamps, chairs, strings of peppers, and every kind of whatnot imaginable. The lady herself was busy in a corner, arranging a display of hand-painted dishes.

"Ms. Nunoz?" I said.

She turned and smiled at me. "Yes?" she asked.

She was a beautiful woman, even prettier than the TV had made her. Her thick black hair was pulled back in a French braid and her dark eyes were made even more striking by the artful application of liner, shadow, and mascara. She was taller than her daughter, but not by much, and her figure was very rounded in all the right places. It was easy to see where Celia had gotten her larger-than-life chest.

"I'm sorry to bother you at work, Ms. Nunoz," I said, "but I wonder if I could talk to you for a moment?"

She frowned and cocked her head. "About what?" she asked.

"Michael Whitby," I said.

Lydia Galeana Nunoz's back straightened ramrod stiff and her eyes blazed at me. "I have nothing to say to you." She turned abruptly and headed into a room marked PRIVATE.

Never having been one to bow to autocratic signs of authority, I followed briskly behind her.

She whirled around when she heard me behind her. "I will call the police if you do not leave at once," she said, her voice low but hard.

"Ms. Nunoz, I'm not a reporter or anything, if that's what you think. I'm just a concerned parent from Black Cat Ridge. I'm sure you're aware of all the trouble we were having with Michael Whitby in our community."

"I have nothing to say to you," she said.

"I know about Celia," I said.

Her face paled. "You know nothing about my daughter. Get out."

"She was totally innocent, just like all the other girls that man accosted—"

"That man never accosted my Celia! He never got near her!"

"I know that, and I'm very glad of it. He was stopped before he could do anything to harm her—or the other girl he was fixated on."

"Other girl?"

"Yes, there was another one. At least one other that I'm aware of." I took a breath. "I know Celia told you about her encounter with Michael Whitby, and I know you told your brother—"

"Where did you hear any of this?" she demanded. "This is my personal life, Miss whoever the hell you are!"

"I'm sorry. E.J. Pu—"

"I don't care who you are!" she said, her voice hard. "I haven't reached where I am today by taking crap from anybody, and I certainly won't take any from you. I want you out of here now!"

"What did Max say when you told him?" I asked, trying to stay my ground.

Lydia Galeana Nunoz frowned, cocking her head again. "Max?"

"Yes. I know you told him. How did he react?"

"What are you talking about?" she demanded.

"Your brother Max—"

She threw her arms up. "Max? Max Galeana? He's not my brother! He's my cousin! I didn't tell

Max anything about this! I wouldn't! He's barely family! He married a gringa!''

"I thought—''

"Well, obviously you don't do that too well, do you?'' she said, arms folded as she smirked at me.

There was a sound from the other side of the door and it opened slowly. A man in an electric wheelchair moved slowly towards us, one finger pressed against the switch that moved the chair.

"Lydia,'' he said, his voice strained as he held his neck at an awkward angle. "You okay?''

"Tomas. Sorry to bother you. This woman was just leaving.''

"I really need to ask you some questions—''

"This is my brother, Tomas,'' Lydia said. "He didn't kill your nasty Mr. Whitby. Neither did I. That is what you wanted to know, isn't it?''

"Ah—''

"So now I suggest you leave. Tomas?''

He moved the chair away from the doorway. I walked through it and out the front door of the shop, heading for the minivan. Okay, so I'd just lost all the grocery money.

I decided to go back to the house and figure out a way to separate Meg from Lord Ashton—so they could get back together again in a frenzy of passion in about another hundred or so pages. I seemed to do better on confrontations with fictional characters.

Carlie Galeana was right: Investigating was boring when nothing was happening. And believe me, nothing was happening. I was beginning to run out of juice. Nobody else seemed to care; by the following

Monday, I'd gotten a call from Arlene Whitby letting me know she got a contract on the house and she and Michael, Jr., would be leaving for Tyler in about a month.

If Arlene didn't care who killed her husband, why should I?

The few times I saw Elena Luna, she was deep in conversation about a supposed drug ring coming out of Black Cat Ridge's high-dollar village. The mention of Michael Whitby's name seemed to bring on nothing more than a suppressed yawn from Luna.

I saw Abby Dane in the grocery store and she passed me as if I were invisible. I started to stop her, but I was totally out of questions. What good would it do?

Nobody seemed to care anymore, if they ever did, about Michael Whitby, Sr. So why should I? The man was dead, the commotion in Black Cat Ridge caused by his life was now over, and no one cared about his death.

Except me.

And even I didn't care that much. I had a book to write, children to feed, a husband to harass, and HCG titers I needed to work on lowering—if I could figure out how to do that.

Life was getting back to as normal as possible—considering I still had a death sentence hanging over my head. Graham and two of his pals got caught tipping cows in a field outside of Black Cat Ridge. The farmer was going to press charges, but decided against it when he discovered one of the boys was the son of a Codderville police detective—namely Elena Luna.

So Graham was confined to his room for two weeks with no Nintendo, no TV, and nothing to read except schoolbooks.

Megan was on a crying jag because Michael, Jr., was moving. Since she'd been his only friend, she'd lost most of her others and was feeling pretty lonely. Bessie came home with a black eye, having gotten in a fight on the playground defending her sister's honor.

All in all, a pretty normal week in the Pugh family.

My appointment with Marta Colman was coming up. The day before, Willis asked me to meet him for lunch in Codderville at the McDonald's. I hadn't been in there since the last time I'd interrogated Mandy Hogkins, another lead that had taken me nowhere in a big hurry.

I parked the minivan and went in, hoping it was early enough that Mandy would still be at school. Willis was sitting at a table with his back to me, already eating his hamburger.

And that's when it hit me.

I knew what had happened. I could see it all. I knew who shot Michael Whitby.

Lee Bowman wasn't the only person in Black Cat Ridge to read Agatha Christie. I'd read my share. And my favorite part had always been the *denouement*.

I made a few phone calls, confided in my husband, who as usual thought I was crazy, got my mother-in-law over to babysit, and that night Willis and I went to Elena Luna's house and rang the bell.

I could hear her boys in the background fighting

over the TV remote, and wondered why Luis hadn't been grounded like Graham, but decided that was really none of my business.

"I have something to show you," I told her.

"What?" she said, looking from me to Willis.

Willis rolled his eyes and shrugged his shoulders, in that way he has of saying, "Just humor her" that I love so much.

I smiled at Luna. "Just come with us," I said.

She grabbed her coat off the hall tree and joined us. We all got in the minivan and headed the few blocks to our destination.

All the cars were there waiting for us. I recognized Lee and Pat Bowman's 4-wheel drive, Abby Dane's Toyota Corolla, the Galeanas' Volvo wagon, and the Perlmutters' Audi. All the lights were blazing in Rene Tillery's house.

We pulled in the driveway behind the Audi and got out.

Keith Tillery answered our knock. "Hey, hey," he said, laughing. "The gang's all here! Come on in. This'll make Rene's month!"

Everyone was in the living room, chairs from the dining room having been pulled in to service. Rene was frantically trying to get drink orders from her unexpected guests.

Then she saw me.

She straightened. "What are you doing here?" she demanded.

I smiled. "Hi, Rene. I'm so glad everyone could make it." Then I said the words I'd been wanting to say my entire life, "I suppose you're all wondering why I called you here."

I grinned. Willis grinned. Elena Luna rolled her eyes. Rene glared.

I took a seat on one of the dining room chairs. "Please," I said, indicating the living room, "everyone sit."

Keith pulled up a chair, Luna perched on the hearth, and Willis sat on the arm of the couch, next to Lee Bowman. Only Rene remained standing.

"What in the hell do you think you're doing?" she asked.

"This is called the *denouement*, right, Lee?" I said.

Lee's eyes got big. "Hey, really?" He grinned and literally rubbed his hands together. "Oh, boy!"

Keith laughed and pulled up another dining room chair. "Come on, honey," he said to his wife. "Sit."

The second Rene sat, I stood up. "Let me begin at the beginning," I said, *à la* Hercule Poirot. "The last time we were all gathered together like this, we had a common goal. To remove Michael Whitby from our midst." I looked around the room, catching as many eyes as I could. Yes, I was having a wonderful time.

"Well, that goal was certainly accomplished. But not in the way I think we had in mind," I said. "Michael Whitby was shot and killed. We all know that. What you may not know," I said, letting the suspense build, "was that he was shot and killed—by someone in this room."

Well, hell. They didn't all look at each other aghast. No furtive looks. No one jumping up and confessing. Actually, three people laughed and one yawned. Of course, the yawner was Luna; what would you expect?

"Something else all of you may not know," I said. "You were all right. Michael Whitby was back to his old tricks. He was stalking a teenaged girl who worked at the McDonald's in Codderville." I decided to leave Celia Nunoz out of the equation—at the moment. "He spent almost every lunch hour there, drove her home, and was building up a fantasy in his mind about the two of them. The girl had no idea what was going on and was not in the least receptive to Whitby's advances.

"But someone in this room didn't know that. Someone in this room saw Michael Whitby every day at the McDonald's. Saw him coming on to the girl. Trying to seduce her. Someone who feared Whitby was going to have his way with another child. Someone in this room who works in Codderville, eats at McDonald's almost every day, who had the opportunity to know what was happening to the girl. I don't believe this person meant to kill Whitby; they probably just wanted to talk with him, but maybe things got out of hand."

"Obviously I knew it could go that way," Keith Tillery said. "I had a gun with me."

Rene stood up. "Shut up, Keith!" she said.

Keith pulled her back down to her seat. "It's okay, honey. The guy was scum. He was seducing another girl. I looked at her and I saw our girls in a few years. I couldn't let it happen again."

I remembered what he'd said to Willis and me at McDonald's that day. "You said we each had to look after our own children. That we were responsible for ourselves—not for the community.''

Keith shrugged. ''And I believe that. It's just that . . . well . . . I saw that little kid, dumb as a post, and Whitby making his moves on her . . .'' He shrugged again. ''I saw him at the McDonald's on Halloween night. I was supposed to be here handing out candy to the trick or treaters, but I wanted a Big Mac. So when Rene and the girls left, I just hopped in the car and drove into Codderville to the drive-in window. I saw him then. Getting out of his car. I knew what he was going to do. I keep a gun in the glove compartment of the car—'' He looked at Luna. ''I'm licensed to carry concealed,'' he said, then grinned, ''so you can't get me for that.

''Anyway, I got out of the car, with the gun, and I met him at the door and pointed the gun at him and told him to get in his car. We drove to his office parking lot. It was quiet there; no one around. And I talked to him. Or tried to. I told him to leave the girl alone, that I knew what he was doing, and he said the girl loved him, and wanted to be with him. He started saying crap like how it wasn't his fault, the girls just came after him, and he knew he shouldn't let them tempt him—crap like that.

''So I said he had to move. Had to leave Black Cat Ridge, and he started getting in my face. No way I was going to drive him out of his home. He had a wife and a kid, blah, blah, blah. And then he just gets out of the car! Just gets out and starts walking back to the McDonald's. So I go after him, and he hits me, and I grab him, and we're acting like total jerks—and then the gun went off.''

"But why did you take him back to his house?" Willis asked. "Why the pumpkin head?"

"Hell, half the people on that block have moved out, and there certainly weren't any kids trick or treating around there. No parent would let their kid within a two-block radius of the Whitby house." He shrugged. "And that bale of hay and a jack-o'-lantern were just sitting there." Keith grinned. "I couldn't help myself."

Rene stood up. "Okay, here's what we do," she said. "I need volunteers to organize a defense fund, I need character witnesses—"

Willis went with me the next day to Marta Colman's office. Marta had promised to get a rush on the blood test.

"You know everything's going to be all right, don't you?" Marta said with a smile while the technician drew the blood.

"Um-hum," I said, with little conviction.

Willis squeezed my shoulder while the technician pulled the needle out and labeled the tube with my blood.

"Y'all go get some breakfast," Marta said. "Be back here by around, what, Lisa," she said, talking to the technician, "about ten-thirty?"

Lisa nodded. "No problem," she said.

Willis and I opted not to go to the McDonald's— too many uncomfortable memories—and instead headed to a diner that served heavy country breakfasts. That was what I needed right now, I decided— serious comfort food. I'd worry about dieting later.

Maybe I'd talk to Carlie Galeana, see what she recommended.

I had ham, eggs, hash browns, and biscuits and tried not to gag when my husband got pancakes with a side of biscuits and gravy. No, he's not carbo-loading. He just does that.

Unfortunately, I couldn't eat. I pushed the food around on my plate and constantly checked my watch. Finally, it was time to head back to Dr. Col-man's office.

She kept us sitting in the waiting room for half an hour. At eleven o'clock we finally were taken back to her office.

"Sit," she said, indicating the two chairs in front of her desk, the big smile indicating what I hoped was good news. "They've gone down," she said.

Willis let out a blast of air, as if he had been holding his breath for the last three weeks, which I'm not sure isn't exactly what he had been doing. I felt tears in my eyes and tried to will them back.

"They're not down as far as they should be," Marta said, "but they appear to be on their way. We'll give it another three weeks. They should be back to normal then."

"If not?" I asked, that old feeling back in the pit of my stomach.

Marta stood and walked toward the door. "E.J., let's celebrate, okay? This is good news. We're not going to have any negative thoughts, okay?"

Easy for her to say, I thought, but didn't say. Instead I just smiled and gave her a hug. "Thanks," I said.

"See you in another three weeks."

Maybe someday life would get back to normal—maybe in just another three weeks.

Arlene Whitby sold the house for a loss, but not a terrible one. She and Mikey moved back to Tyler, Texas. They came by to see us the day before they left, and Megan and Bessie cried to see Mikey go. He was very big about it and gave each girl a kiss on the cheek before he and his mother left. Graham, who had been allowed downstairs finally, rolled his eyes and made a gagging noise, but all in all, it was a touching moment.

Megan seems to be gradually working her way back into the good graces of her old friends, so things should be getting back to normal there, although backing Michael, Jr., did have a positive effect on the relationship between my two daughters. It was the old, "I can say whatever I want about my sister, but you do and I'll knock your block off" scenario.

The last time I talked to Luna, she said Keith Tillery and his lawyer were working out a plea with the district attorney. She said the DA was afraid if the case went before a jury they'd award Keith a cash settlement for community service. She said the chances of Keith spending time in jail were nil. The powers that be were going to treat this as a "misdemeanor murder," and nobody really cared. The real threat to the community, they figured, had been Michael Whitby, not Keith Tillery.

But I couldn't help wondering what would happen if another felon moved to Black Cat Ridge? Would the fact that Keith had literally gotten away with murder spur others on to dispose of any similar problem in a quick and painless—for the community at least—way?

Luna and I discussed this at some length, but neither of us came up with any answers.

I still wasn't particularly popular with Rene, Tina, or Abby, but Carlie and I were becoming friends and Lee and Pat Bowman called a little more often than I would like.

Meg discovered her true royal birth and she and Lord Ashton were married—after a lot of really good sex—and lived happily ever after. The manuscript is in the mail.

The HCG levels went back down to normal. Marta Colman said I had to have the levels checked every six months—probably for the rest of my life.

Meanwhile, we decided it was definitely time to do something permanent about birth control. Willis actually made the appointment himself. Two weeks before Christmas I drove him to the doctor. Willis had spent the night before on the phone with every man he knew who'd had the procedure, all of them pumping him up for the experience.

It was a Friday. After lying in bed all weekend, he was supposed to be okay for work on Monday. Of course the doctor who predicted this didn't realize my husband needs a local for a haircut.

The waiting room was empty when we got there. Willis fidgeted, actually picking up a copy of *Cosmo* as if he were going to read it. Finally the nurse came and called his name. I stood up, kissed him, and watched him walk slowly towards the door to his doom.

I sat in the reception room waiting. I read the *Cosmo*, *Field and Stream*, and was into a three-week-old *Newsweek* when the outer door of the reception room opened. A small woman came in, pulling behind her a very large, very scared man. She was saying, "It's gonna be okay, honey, really." The man produced no actual words—just moans.

At that moment Willis came out, walking carefully. I stood up. "Hey, honey, how'd it go?" I asked, moving toward him.

And my husband, always one for the witty rejoinder, said, in a high, squeaky falsetto, "Oh, just fine."

The big man who had been coming in the door jerked his arm out of his wife's grasp and ran for the parking lot. The woman shot Willis a mean look and headed after him.

We laughed all the way home.